KLEM WATERCREST

The Lighthouse Keeper

Written and Illustrated by

JAY DIEDRECK

ISBN 978-1-64114-552-7 (paperback)
ISBN 978-1-64114-553-4 (digital)

Christian Faith Publishing, Inc.
832 Park Avenue
Meadville, PA 16335
www.christianfaithpublishing.com

Printed in the United States of America

To my loving wife, Alicia.

Contents

Chapter 1

Klem, Jane, Sarah, Burton, and Lester

In the year of our Lord, 1960

KLEM WATERCREST SAT IN HIS 1950s decorated New England kitchen watching his lovely wife, a marriage of ten years. Jane Watercrest paused for a moment to wipe her forehead using the back of her hand before pulling the sweet rolls out of the black-and-white porcelain gas oven. Over the years, very little was updated in their sweet, little home. Of course, the oven and refrigerator were replaced, not because of Klem's wish however. Jane kept her desire for a new, larger, and updated refrigerator at the forefront of Klem's mind. Jane learned various light but effective techniques that she perfected over the years for what she needed.

Using this technique not too long ago, Jane asked Klem, "Hey, big guy. Can you get some ice cream from the freezer, and I will make some scrumptious root beer floats for both of us? No need to tell the kids about this. They would not approve." Now, Klem was a simple man but had a great weakness for a nice root beer float. Rising from his well-worn dark burgundy leather recliner and heading toward the kitchen, he could see the root beer float in his mind's eye. Almost real, he envisioned two nicely placed scoops of ice cream, suspended just under the light brown foam that was majestically spilling over the side of his favorite frosted mug. A long-handled silver spoon was pushed into the creamy smooth vanilla ice cream mass. He swallowed several times in anticipation. Just as Klem's fingers touched the refrigerator's chrome handle, Jane said using perfect calculation with her words, "Oh, Klem. I tried to find a place in the freezer for ice cream, but it's too small. We only had room for frozen lima beans. So sorry, my love! Would you like lima beans instead? By the way, since you are in the kitchen, the refrigerator needs to be defrosted again. I'll boil some water for you if you want me to."

Soon after this, Klem decided to purchase a new refrigerator that had a large freezer for lima beans and vanilla ice cream.

Jane loved black-and-white checkered patterns, and their bright sunny kitchen boasted of some pretty ribbons on her jars as well as hand-stenciled checkered pattern borders along the walls near the ceiling. This morning, through the kitchen bay window, Klem could see the very top of the lighthouse on the bluff, about a seven-minute walk away. This lighthouse was constructed having eighteen-inch walls of fieldstone and lime mortar. Its exterior displayed a sea-spray-weathered white stucco hue.

Twenty-five years ago, Lester, the previous gentleman who kept the lighthouse maintained and working, finally could not manage the staircase of seventy-two steps leading to the lamphouse at the top. His poor wobbly legs were just plain worn out after years of carrying the heavy kerosene oil bucket to the top landing of the black metal winding staircase. The glowing wick inside the fourth-order Fresnel lens asked to be constantly fed with kerosene. The lens, a collection of perfectly placed glass prisms arranged in a vertical hollow column, also had to be wiped clean of soot and salt-laden sea spray. Even this task required the old gentleman to stand on a four-foot wooden step ladder, perched on the top landing. The task required two or more hours every week. The upper rows of glass prisms were a reach of eight feet, hardly a minor cleaning task. On a clear evening, this lens projected a light beam from the little wick flame as far as three miles to sea. History would prove that it was Lester who, on his first day of work, named the lighthouse "Gray Cliff Light." The name never changed over many years.

So, Lester, with great emotions and heavy heart, knew he would have to make his announcement at the next monthly village meeting. He would have to give up his lifelong dedication to the only lady of his life—his pride and joy of stucco, stone, glass, and iron.

Klem liked going to these village meetings where everyone had a chance to speak. To him, it was the epitome of the American representation, which is still alive in his perfect seaside little village of Port James. Anyone could bring up his or her concern or topic to the front of the group, as long as they got on the agenda no later than four business days prior to the meeting. Sarah Tucker, the wife of Burton Tucker, owner of the town's hardware store, appropriately called "Burton's," was in charge of organizing the agenda for each Tuesday, every month. Some asked why Sarah took on this duty, but most assumed that it was because, quite frankly, no one else wanted the job. Village meetings were always held on the third Tuesday of the month. The origin for meeting on that calendar day was unclear, but it was never challenged, so it stayed on Tuesdays, promptly at 6:30 p.m.

Most in attendance walked from their homes to the meeting place that was held in the back of the public library, a stone and brick building looking similar to a small, European town courthouse. The interior was simple, the benches were wooden, the windows were made of pane glass squares, and the podium upfront where the villagers addressed their neighbors and friends was Shaker style except for the Port James Village logo. This library back room boasts a seating capacity of no more than sixty-five people; the fire marshal's sign stated just that. Complying with village ordnances, the sign had to be at least one foot square having three-inch letters and must be prominently posted. In this case, just inside the vestibule was acceptable so said Nick, the fire marshal.

So, on that particular evening, Lester, the lighthouse keeper, was on the agenda and had a maximum of fifteen minutes to speak, although he knew that that was much more than enough. Holding back tears with only partial success, Lester meandered up to the podium and looked at his friends in the room. With passion coming from a man dedicated to his pride and joy, Lester delivered his message to the small gathering.

Klem admired Lester immensely; and now, he was watching poor Lester, his knees knocking together, not from stage fright but from the wear of old age. Lester had performed his tour of duty well, and there was nothing more for him to do but make his short announcement that would completely change his life. As Lester gazed over his friends from the platform, something moved his spirit to talk from his heart. After a long uncomfortable pause, Lester gathered his thoughts.

"My fellow citizens… no that's not it. Let me start again, my neighbors and friends, I'm not so good with words, so I would like to quote my feelings to all of you from the theme song of my favorite radio program called *Friendship*."

Lester cleared his throat and continued,

I call you my friends
Each day we begin
A feeling of love and sharing.
You keep me close
For which I love most
My Friends, I know you are caring.

In reality, Lester was not on the top of anyone's list to a party, but it didn't matter to him. This was the way Lester felt. Everyone in this village was his friend even if no words were spoken, and to be sure except for this very moment, words of expression were not one of his strengths. He had no time for gossip, and he would not speak ill of anyone. Because of this simple philosophy, anyone he encountered in his seventy years of life was, in his mind, his friend. Maybe this was too simple for most people to live by, but it didn't matter; in Lester's mind, this outlook suited him and served him in life just fine.

Lester looked out through his scratched bifocal glasses at the group, took a deep breath, and headed down from the platform away from the podium. As he walked, he instinctively looked down at his footsteps, a learned habit from ascending and descending the lighthouse's winding staircase. In silence, he found his humble seat nearly at the last row of the room. There was a long, silent pause in the meeting room after Lester sat down. Sarah, standing against the wall to the left of the meeting room, started to clap her hands. There was no party for Lester, and he wanted it that way. His eyes filled up with salty tears, however, when everyone joined in the applause. He knew he was among friends.

After the village meeting and arriving home again, Sarah talked to her husband while sharing some decaffeinated coffee and cookies in their dining room. Sarah was a stickler about using their formal dining room every day if possible.

During the Christmas season, the dining table served as a Christmas present wrapping center as well as a place to sign and address Christmas cards. Sarah had a list of people who gave them a card every year. If, after two years, they did not receive a card from an individual, they were taken off the master list. So, for several weeks, the dining room was not used for eating, however only during that time. Sarah wanted to use every room.

"Why," she would say, "it would be just a complete and utter waste of craftsmanship and raw materials that our God had supplied this earthly world *not* to use my dining room! And look at all this nice glassware. By golly, we are going to use everything, our water pitcher, our English plate settings, our good silverware. You know very well my Burton, after we die, our kids won't care about these things. They want everything new."

Catching a cookie crumb from his mouth, Burton stated, "Honey, you have that far-off look again in your eyes. I would like to know what you are planning, but frankly am afraid to ask."

"Burton, we have to do something for Lester. We just must. He worked at that old Gray Lady lighthouse for so many years, and what did we do for him? After a minute, we gave him an applause. Big deal! Oh, Burton, I failed someone who considers all of us his friends! What was I thinking? I knew he was going to make the announcement of his retirement, but I just wasn't thinking. I'm so ashamed of myself!"

Burton knew he was several pages behind his wife's thought and her agony and therefore decided not to ask for another cookie just yet.

"Well, my lovely wife, I can make a very nice plaque for Lester. And we can present it at our next village meeting."

With this act of kindness, Burton felt deserving of another cookie. "Honey, may I have another chocolate chip cookie?"

"Why, Burton, you can finish the whole dish! What a lovely idea you have!"

Burton thought that "lovely" was not a very macho idea for any man to have but decided not to break his advantage. He just had a smile for his wife as he partook of three more of the delicious morsels from the small English serving plate.

"The only thing I was thinking big guy…"

Gosh, Burton thought, how can a woman think so quickly of so many things in such a rapid fire as she? He was still only at the time and place of the plaque idea, and who knows where she is now.

"What are you thinking of now, darling?"

Tapping her fingers on the table, Sarah replied, "I think it took poor Lester all his effort he could muster to make that announcement tonight. Instead of a formal presentation at a Tuesday village meeting, I believe he would appreciate you and me presenting the plaque to him at his home. What do you think?"

Burton took a moment to admire Sarah's insight. She is certainly right.

"Yes, dear. You have his own feelings in mind. You are right. Could I have some more coffee?"

Burton had a well-equipped workshop in the back of his hardware store where he could fix almost any household problem, anything from window screens to toasters. His woodworking tools were basic—a small table saw, jigsaw, electric drill, some hand chisels, and his father's brace and bit that was given to him years ago. A lot of finished projects came out of Burton's back room. Burton liked to talk through handyman problems with some mighty fine but clueless customers and took adequate time with each of them. One day, after wandering around the plumbing isle for almost a half hour, George Timer finally came to the front counter with a handful of bathroom faucet parts.

Burton said, "That looks like a Saturday morning project if ever I have seen one. Does Linda know you will have to shut off the water for a while?"

"Oh, sure. I got that all covered, Burton. It shouldn't take too long at all."

Burton learned over the years as a small hardware owner to use controlled tack to keep his customers from going to the big box store. He gave a little smile before speaking.

"George, is this bathroom spigot the original one that came with your house?"

Looking at his pile of washers, plumber's putty, and something else that looked like a bishop from a brass chess set, George mustered a weak and hopeless "yes."

"I hope you don't mind me saying that some people would find the job a little easier if you used the black rubber replacement washers I have in that drawer at the beginning of the isle where you were just looking. Would you want me to assist you?

George responded, "Sure why not. Just don't tell my wife I needed your help. She still thinks I am her hero."

"Your secret is safe. Anything for continued marital bliss! George, there are several sizes of washers. But since I know the age of your house plumbing, I think the 5/8-inch flattop black neoprene washer will work. If by chance, it doesn't, you can always return them. I'll put back this brass item you don't need. That is for a Kitchen Master brand gas stove fitting."

So, in between customers when the store was quiet, Burton had the ability to stare in any direction and visualize how to put together more complicated projects. Once, he had all the pieces laid out in his mind in blueprint fashion to construct a wooden secretary rolltop desk. In comparison, this plaque for Lester would be rather easy. Burton envisioned the finished project size to be about five by eight inches and made of black walnut with either a copper or brass engraved plate on the face.

Chapter 2

Lester's Little Gift

THE WEATHER IN PORT JAMES was finally turning the corner, as people say. Spring had delivered softer temperature mornings, and even now, crocuses of purple and white were pushing through the remaining snow to show their faces. There might be another two or three snowfalls before April was finished; but the sun, now higher in the day sky, will surely melt the snow after an hour's time.

It was this morning at the breakfast table that Sarah and Burton were sharing their ideas for their day's activities. It was Monday, and Burton took Mondays off from the store. Burton's hardware store on Mondays was staffed by his cousin, who knew his way around fix-it projects, a little. If in a bind, he knew it would be best to call Burton instead of giving out wayward advice.

"Burton, my dear, I called Lester while you were in the shower and asked him if we could stop by his house around ten o'clock today. So besides going for a little walk along the bluff, and this visit, that is all I have for today."

"Well, Sarah, I think I will go for a second cup of java, and then, I will be all set to go."

Lester's home, a three-minute walk from the Tuckers, was made of cobblestone and trimmed with pale yellow southern pinewood boards. Over 130 years old like most of the village homes, it was also modestly small but efficient especially for a single older gentleman. Burton twisted the round mechanical bell attached to the front door.

The clapper inside the bell spun, making a ging! ging!, sounding like a little girl's old-fashioned bicycle bell.

Lester opened his door and motioned them to enter the foyer area of the living room. He seemed friendly but a little concerned about their visit. After entering, Lester hobbled to his multicolored Tiffany table lamp and switched it on by pulling its little metal chain.

"Welcome, Sarah and Burton. You really did not have to call ahead of time to come over. Since retiring from the lighthouse duties, I'm home most of the time now."

Sarah nodded in an understanding way.

"On behalf of the whole community, children and adults alike, and those out-of-state tourists on lighthouse hunts, we would like to present this "Thank You" plaque for all your years of dedication and hard, endless work. We hope whoever takes over the lighthouse duties will fashion their job after you. Lester, you are both a good man and good lighthouse keeper."

With that short speech, Sarah handed the plaque to Burton and Burton handed it to Lester. Without hesitation, he received the gift with both hands and admired it greatly, turning it left and right, getting the best view of it. Lester's hands were rough and cracked; little black lines of soot outlined his fingerprints like a tattoo of time and arduous work. With a soft "thank you," Lester propped his brass and wooden reward on the center of his fireplace mantle.

"Friends, this is very kind of you. I didn't expect this. Please also thank everyone who scribed their signatures on the back. I do thank you so very much."

Each and every day, for the rest of Lester's three years on this earth, he would touch the side or corner of his plaque. He would read each name as he walked past the fireplace mantle. His favorite place in his small five-room home was the front room where his reclining chair was located. From this advantage point, Lester could see his fireplace mantle, his plaque, and his eighteen-inch black-and-white Zenith television. Gazing through his wavy glass front window, he could look outside and admire his wisteria. The wisteria grew to reach the top of his arched arbor, which greeted visitors from the front sidewalk. For the most part, Lester was a happy soul, mostly because he accepted his failing abilities instead of fretting over any old-age shortcomings.

Chapter 3

Sweet Rolls and a New Keeper of the Light

So, THIS MORNING, ONCE AGAIN, Klem couldn't take his eyes off the sweet rolls, their aroma filled his spirit. They were better tasting than any lady's in the village, probably because they were made of the best ingredients and, of course, made with love.

Jane, holding the baking sheet of sweet rolls, walked past Klem and paused just briefly to give her husband of ten years a naughty wink. She lowered the baking sheet on two pot holders that she had placed on the tiled counter next to the porcelain sink.

"Hey, big boy, do you want some?"

Klem was salivating for the rolls, but his heart was tickled inside when Jane was a little playful with him, especially when it was unexpected.

"May I partake of some of your sweetness, my dear?" Klem continued the playfulness.

"Well, my most deserving hunk, I thought you would never ask." And with that, Jane lightly and purposely brushed Klem's shoulder as she joined him at the kitchen table."

"Goodness, gracious, great wonderful flow of happiness, my good woman, these are heavenly! In fact, I do believe that these are the very sweet rolls that they serve in heaven!"

And with that, showing kind of a military flare with his hands, Klem placed another warm sweet roll on his blue-and-white pattern plate.

"Good Lord, what did I do to deserve this fine woman?" Klem had a habit of conversing with himself this way quite often.

This perfect twinkle of time, the kind of moment in one's life that could be easily overlooked if one did not take notice that it truly was perfect, vanished as quickly as it came. Klem and Jane's front door knocker made several hollow thumps against the door's raised floating panel. Jane was already standing, and with another wink of promise to Klem, she walked to the door to answer the knock. Standing on the outside brick walkway so Jane could see her better was Sarah. She definitely was on a mission. Jane surmised she was most likely going to ask for some sort of input for Tuesday's community meeting's agenda.

"Hi, Jane, and good morning to you."

With her right hand holding a rolled-up sheet of white typing paper and pen, she greeted Jane with a hug, patting Jane's back lightly.

"Jane, is Klem in and able to talk to for a few minutes? Actually, I think it would be good if I could talk to both of you since it involves you both."

"Sure, Sarah. Klem and I were just finishing breakfast and watching the sunrise come up through the kitchen bay window. Come on into the kitchen. You can see the lighthouse almost glow with pink and orange colors from the sky. This happens just for a few minutes this time of the day. Is the kitchen table okay for you?"

"Oh sure, that will be just fine. Hello, Klem."

"Hello, Sarah. How's Burton? I think I will need a new screen put in the back door before summer comes."

Placing her reading glasses on her nose, Sarah looked at both Klem and Jane and then started to flatten down her rolled-up paper agenda onto the table.

"Well, my friends, I am sure you were as surprised as many about Lester's last month's village meeting announcement. He just could not keep up, and as you know because you were there, he had to step down as lighthouse keeper of Gray Cliff Light. I thought about this since his announcement and would like you, Klem, to think about taking up the duty. As you know, it is a full-time job. And much of the pay you receive is in the knowledge that you are both part of nautical history, fine tradition, and an important part of saving the lives of sailors at sea."

Sarah thought she would let this sink in and not say another word no matter how long the silence. Klem shuffled his body in his chair a few times, and only the faint squeaking of chair legs could be heard. Jane was looking at her Klem, thinking that he was only forty years old and could serve in this capacity for twenty-five or more years. He kept himself fit. He and Jane walked whenever it was possible even on errands such as going to the corner market for fresh produce or items to make her sweet rolls.

However lucky, Klem had inherited genes that required little effort to keep a slim figure. In fact, as a boy, he was severely under-weight. When picking teams for touch football in high school gym class, he would always be last. In fact, sometimes, the team leaders would just ignore he was in the class. Klem would just silently join either team on his own. Now, however, as other men his age were growing pot bellies, he could eat anything and look good, even in a bathing suit.

Jane was the first to speak. "Klem, I know this will affect both of us. But whatever you decide, I will be by your side. Just don't make the wrong decision!"

At first, Klem thought her response was going his way until her last emphatic statement. Just don't make the wrong decision? What was going through her head to say this?

Klem grew up along the coast of Maine and loved to visit and learn about lighthouses. In many ways, Sarah's request was a dream come true, no matter how hard the job was. Klem could feel the excitement well up inside—the thought of being a lighthouse keeper! Little beads of sweat joined his increasing heartbeat, and his faster breathing was almost uncontrollable. Well, he thought, this was not the time to misconstrue anything in his short marriage with Jane. He needed to be sure of her statement. He didn't want to disappoint her.

"Jane, I need to ask you what did you mean, just don't make the wrong decision?"

"'Klem, Klem, Klem, listen to me carefully."

Jane got up and walked over to put her hands on his shoulders from behind his chair.

"I love you. The very wrong decision you might make would be basing it on what you think I want. That would truly be wrong."

Jane walked around Klem, now facing him. She placed her hand on top of her husband's. He looked into her hazel eyes, those eyes he fell in love with. Gosh, he could have gotten lost in her eyes. Those beautiful eyes had taught him of her happiness or sadness. With this man, her eyes could not possibly hide how she felt. This time, Klem saw another feeling in her eyes, that of complete sincerity. She said what she meant, and now, she sincerely meant what she said.

Sarah knew not to disrupt their union just yet but instead gave them some time. Over the years of asking people for various volunteer work, she knew she needed to eventually speak but only at the appropriate time.

"Klem and Jane, don't give me an answer now. Give it a while and talk it over. Take all the time you need, as long as you give me an answer *before Tuesday*."

The threesome laughed at her statement, and then, Jane took the hint that this meeting was over. Sarah rolled up her agenda once again as she rose from her chair and headed toward the door.

At the next Tuesday village meeting, the room was about half full. More souls might have made it, but April rains dampened the number. Sarah brought up several items of community interest for majority vote or rejection.

"Thank you all for coming on this rainy evening. The first item of business is the annual garage sale. It is a 50/50 sale once again at the White Church. Pastor Steel will have the parking lot available, and half of what is made goes to the church Altar Guild. For those who may not know, the Altar Guild pays for funeral flowers, bread and wine for Holy Communion, altar cloths, and the occasional banners and candles. It is important for them to have enough money especially for candles because last year, they ran out of money just before Christmas.

Most of you know this story of last year. To save a little money, the Pastor allowed the eternal flame candle to burn down a little too much. Right in the middle of Pastor Steel's sermon on church giving, the eternal flame candle sputtered a few times then completely burned out for all to witness. We can't have something like that happening again, whether you are Lutheran, Congregationalist, or whatever."

A vote was taken, and the garage sale was approved for July 22.

"The next order of business is the temporary filling of the huge pothole outside of the IGA. Now, we know the village road crew will be filling it properly in June when the asphalt will be warm enough to stay together. But right for now, about a yard of crushed stone is needed. Tom from the village said that a yard should be enough, and he would be willing to do the job if we could buy the stone. His budget is set, and there is no money for stone especially if it is used for a temporary fix. After all that heavy rain we have been having, poor Lady Dollson had quite an unfortunate mishap.

While walking her standard poodle, Mark, the poor dog fell in the pothole brim full of rain water, almost pulling Lady Dollson right in with her dog. What a commotion both made. Lady broke her left black high heels on one of her favorite dress shoes. Besides all this, she got a grand run in her stockings. If it wasn't for Walt, our Port James news reporter, pulling old Mark out of the mess, Lady would have been in there too. Of course, since Walt couldn't pass up a good story, the whole incident made the first page of the paper, complete with colored photos. The next day, Walt ended up with such a back sprain that he was required by his doctor to have a full two weeks of bed rest. And besides, we all know his heart is not all that good. So, with all that, may we have a vote to use our sunshine fund to purchase the crushed stone?"

Everyone except Hank Lowell voted "yes." Hank never liked Lady Dollson's dog singing from his back yard, which was right outside Hank's bedroom window. Nor did Hank like that this same dog felt the urge to sing soprano at four o'clock every morning. Poor Hank needed his sleep to do his job right at his one-man gas station.

Sarah took her rolled-up paper, flattened it down on the podium one more time, and announced the final item.

"So, this brings us to the final item on tonight's agenda. We should be able to get you home early before this rain comes down more earnestly. I approached our dear friend and neighbor Klem Watercrest a couple of days ago. I asked him whether he would have the desire to become the lighthouse keeper of Gray Cliff Light now that Lester has retired. Yesterday, Klem, by the way, could you stand up please? Klem gave it some heartfelt consideration, and even after some prayer (he told me so), decided he would be honored to become the keeper of the Gray Cliff Light. As a formality, we need to ask if anyone else would like the job, and if so, we should bring it to a vote."

Without any further discussion to the contrary, Sarah brought the vote to the floor and Klem was made Lester's successor as lighthouse keeper. Now immediately, it became Klem's occupation, "keeper of the light" for this grand old lady of the seas. Besides the keeper of the light, Klem will have the responsibility to maintain the structure, which was at one time the keeper's home right next to the light. Now, this home has been converted into a museum and gift shop.

Chapter 4

Klem Watercrest

So KLEM WAS A PRETTY happy man. His wife cared for him deeply, a true gift of God as he would tell his buddies from church. Some of these gentlemen made their livelihood by the sea. Yes, they agreed with Klem, except he was "extra blessed" having Jane's talents in the kitchen paralleling her love for him. Klem would say to his buddies, "I met Jane when I was 138 pounds and had a thirty-inch waist. Now, I have a forty-inch waist and sporting a frame of 170 pounds. Now, that is a lot of love."

On the first day of Klem's new duty, he asked if Jane would make him some blueberry pancakes. Every August, Jane handpicked Maine blueberries from the old abandoned fruit orchard just off the dirt road, named Terry's Pass. The road, if one could still call it, runs east and west along the other side of Port James a few miles away. It used to be a stagecoach path in its day.

One hundred plus years ago, parts of the road were privately owned and maintained. The family who maintained the road also manned a booth and gate to collect a small toll, usually three cents. The gate was called a pike. Some crafty stagecoach drivers would go way around the pike to save the toll. From that came the name "turnpike."

The fruit farm did well as it also was a stagecoach stop, restaurant, hotel and grill, a friendly place for weary travelers to take a meal, and an overnight before continuing further on their destinations.

"Klem, slow down. No one is going to steal it from you, darling!" With that said, Jane reached over to him once more, this time touching his back lightly with her hand as if she needed to balance. With her kitchen flipper, she slid his fourth blueberry pancake onto his black and white square plate. The masterpiece was not without much butter and maple syrup sinking in slightly on the top and onto the plate. Jane's plate was mismatched from the rest. Hers is a commemorative 150-year anniversary plate for their "Our Lord's Lutheran Church" and had a sketch of the church facade.

Klem liked the ambience of the stained-glass windows in Our Lord's Lutheran Church, especially the rose window above the white altar. The rose window was not like the normal rose windows found in the huge cathedrals having intricate patterns of many colored glass pieces. This small church contained seating for only 122 souls and had its roots deep within the lives of the fishing community. The round stained-glass window above the altar depicted a merchant schooner under full sail, fighting to stay upright at night within an angry gray and turbulent ocean. Only partly visible was a section of a lighthouse like the one to which Klem had dedicated his new occupation. It was visible from the starboard side of the ship.

Klem may have been the only parishioner who saw within its scene something even more marvelous. Every year, on the longest day of summer, "summer solstice," June 21, if the sky was clear, the morning sun would find itself coming through the stained-glass window of Our Lord's Lutheran Church in a most inspirational way. This short-lived celestial phenomenon occurred at exactly 10:15 a.m. It would light up the lighthouse in the stained-glass window, casting a guiding beam of light toward the ship at sea—the ship in peril. Klem thought that this was a true sign from his creator. The ship in the scene would safely glide into port without any sailors being lost in that evening storm.

The pastor of Our Lord's Lutheran Church, Pastor Dell, was a brilliant man, with an understanding well past his thirty-nine years of life. He had been a pastor of only this parish, and he loved each member of his church. He arrived straight from the seminary at the ripe age of twenty-six, full of ambition and hoping to increase this church's membership two- or threefold. After all, being a successful pastor was totally related to his ability to increase the membership, right? However, that was not to be after all. These numbers were fine with Pastor Dell's Lord and Savior, but not with Pastor Dell.

One Sunday, after the church service, Klem saw this talented young pastor obsessing once again about church membership numbers. This number game was something Pastor Dell mentioned in the sermon several times. Klem decided to chat with the good pastor over coffee. During the summer months, coffee hour was held in the church's small backyard terrace garden. The terrace was made of redbrick laid in a herringbone pattern. This redbrick terrace installed by the board of trustees with Burton's help was only two years old.

"Such a nice eye appeal," said most of the men parishioners, but the women liked it much more.

"Now, us women won't get our high heels stuck in the grass every time we gather out back during coffee hour."

So once again, during this coffee hour on the terrace, Klem noticed the pastor sitting on the border of the brick, obsessing over membership numbers.

With the loving tack that Klem provided as second nature, and not something he planned ahead for, he walked over to Pastor Dell. He placed his hand on the overworked pastor's shoulder.

"Pastor Dell, my good man, may I mention what the Lord thinks is a successful career for any man of the cloth?"

Klem spoke as if God himself had revealed this to him face to face. He continued, "Pastor Dell, God will judge your success if you only saved just a single soul for His own. My friend, you have certainly accomplished that."

After looking into Klem's steel gray eyes as if he was seeing God himself, Pastor Dell thanked him and was at peace ever since receiving that simple gift of Klem's religious insight.

No one truly knows who and how many souls the Holy Spirit has touched through each and every one of us. It is not only delivered from the pulpit. No one knows when or where, but it could happen in any of our daily lives. Klem had always tried to grasp any opportunity to share his religious faith when someone needed God's helping hand.

Chapter 5

Our Daily Lives

TURNING TO THE TASKS THAT had to be done to keep the lighthouse broadcasting its beam into the night sky, Klem took his can of kerosene and started up the winding staircase. With every step he took, climbing higher and higher, Klem would say each word of the Lord's Prayer. The first phrase of the prayer "Our Father who art in heaven" would take six steps. Quite conveniently, the Lord's Prayer was seventy-two words long, and the lighthouse's step count was exactly seventy-two. Including the lamphouse at the top, the lighthouse was a little under six stories high from the ground. As Klem's spiritual routine continued, once at the top, he would go directly past the fourth-order Fresnel lens in the lamphouse through the short doorway onto the narrow outside ledge. With one hand on the rail, Klem would gaze at the New England scene below.

With each direction of the compass, he saw four distinct activities. First to the east was the mighty sea, south was the boat-building shipyard, west were the farmlands, and north was the Port James's war memorial. He would say a short but sincere prayer at each direction. In the east, he prayed for the safety of those sailors at sea. Toward the south, he prayed for the men and women working at the ship-building yards.

From previous tours of the yards, he remembered the steel hulls, the sounds of welding, grinding, and riveting. Against the huge hulls, the workmen looked like little ants. Some hung perilously from a small bench on a rope swing making boats and making a living. Some had dreams for their children, and some dreamed of having children. The fortunate ones would come home safely having families who loved them, rejoicing when arriving back home.

To the west again, he prayed for the safety of those operating any farm machinery such as harvesters, bailers, tillers, and even the farm animals. The Port James's war memorial was a reminder for Klem to pray for the safety for all service men and women, as well as good government for all the villages, towns, counties, states, and politicians in Washington DC. Sometimes, one prayer was longer than the other, depending on what was happening in the news.

So yes, in many ways, not only was this a place of employment for Klem, a lighthouse structure that needed continuous attention, but also it was his sanctuary, his church away from church.

Then, as usual, he took out his paper towels and Windex and scrubbed the gulls's calling cards from the outside of the lighthouse windows. Once back inside, Klem would tip the kerosene bucket with its long gooseneck and carefully direct the fluid, filling the container where the cloth wick would feed. The guiding beam of light that brought boats safely home would continue again for another night. The kerosene lantern floated on a puddle of liquid mercury, which allowed it to rotate in a circle with ease. The complete rotation of every fifty-five seconds was driven by weights on a chain just like a grandfather's clock.

The small flame from the kerosene lantern would not be seen more than a few hundred feet if it wasn't for the Fresnel lens. A Fresnel lens is a beautiful arrangement of solid glass prisms that makes a column around the flame. With an aid of a shiny six-inch circular concave mirror on one side of the wick flame and the glass prisms totaling forty-six in all, the beam streaming from Klem's lighthouse could be seen for three miles or more.

Chapter 6

Life Goes On

Seasons come and seasons go and years pile up recording the history of time, pages in a history book. Klem and Jane truly felt that time wasn't a constant. It truly seemed to go faster as they grew older. Sundays came quicker and quicker, but how could this be?

Klem was already sixty-five years old now. He had been the Gray Cliff Lighthouse keeper for twenty-five years. He and Jane had been married for thirty-five years. Thinking about the outside world, it seemed to him that technology became more complicated as he grew older. Why did a coffee percolator have to have a computer inside, and worst yet, why did the new owner have to program it before the first cup? Klem knew that in these days with ships and small boats alike are equipped with GPS systems. His beloved lighthouse was secondary at best for safe navigation. It certainly was his hope that the politicians whom he prayed for would not let this marvel become dark any day soon, but that might happen sooner than he wanted.

Klem started his descent down the seventy-two steps of the lighthouse from the lamphouse at the top. Upon emerging back into the sunlight from the dark winding staircase, he saw Hank sitting on the wooden and metal bench near the lighthouse entrance. Klem walked over to Hank who was looking down, his head almost between his legs.

"Hank, what is wrong? Are you all right?"

Hank, fumbling for the right words and seeming pretty distraught, managed to ask Klem for a few minutes of his time. Klem knew from Hank's body language and concerned look on his face that this may be another one of God's opportunity for him.

"Hank, I will always have time for you. Let me clean myself up a little inside the gift shop, and I will be right out. Don't go anywhere."

Hank owned the first, oldest, and only gas station in town. Years before the gas station was installed holding tanks and gas pumps, it was a store that sold all kinds of nautical wares imaginable. There was always a steady stream of sailors who could find their needs met without ever having to leave town. Without this merchant, the nearest nautical supply was located in Port Smith, a good ninety minutes south one way. After being at sea for sometimes a half a year, deckhands and various mariners could get the parts for repairs right in town, thus more time for either family, drinking, or both.

Waiting for Klem to come back, Hank was thinking about his life, a life that now was falling apart. It seemed like only a moment away when his son Tom would help him at the gas station. It has been a good twelve years or more since Tom walked after school dismissal to his dad's gas station. There, he would find his dad working on a car or pumping some fuel.

Tom would greet his father who then would give his son two quarters to buy a soda and candy bar from the waiting room vending machines. With his snack in one hand and his book bag in the other, Tom would prop himself in the gas station's front bay window to mull over his homework. Having his dad nearby in the waiting room or working in one of the two car bays of the station made him an easy target for math questions. Hank would anguish over what seemed like endless math homework questions Tom brought home from school.

"Dad, when you have a chance, can you help me with this? I have already tried to work this problem five times from Sunday, and I still don't get it."

"For crying out loud in a bucket, Tom, didn't they go over that in school?"

Tom never cried in a bucket like his dad's favorite expression announced, but he got the idea that his dad was a little exasperated whenever he said it.

"Dad, I truly think the teacher doesn't even understand it. That's why they ask us to do it for them, as homework for us."

"Tom, I don't think... whatever. Let's see the darn thing."

Wiping his black greased hands on his mechanic's cloth that he kept in his back pocket of his Carhartt one-piece overalls, Hank brought his attention to the homework that was presented to him. Sitting next to his son on the bench of the bay window, Hank stared at the word problem, while Tom pulled down the wrapper of his Babe Ruth candy bar, his soda near his side. Tom loved having a dad who would be there to help him. He never knew, however, that his all-knowing dad was using every bit of gray brain matter he had to work through something called "new math."

Why in tarnation couldn't these schools keep math the good old way we all learned it? After all, most of the 178 years of Port James's school graduates were successful. They had their own homes, raised their families, and sent their children off on their own to continue another chapter in their lives—all without this confounded new math.

So, years later, here was Hank, not at his gas station, but ready to meet Klem at the base of the white stucco lighthouse. Hank was carrying sadness in his soul.

Klem came out of the lighthouse gift shop catching the screen door with his arm so it would not startle Hank with a bang when it pulled shut. Klem felt the importance of this meeting but could not conclude anything quite yet.

"Hi, Klem, I, uh, I…can you sit with me here on your bench for a few? I need to gather my thoughts a little."

Klem welcomed these few moments of silence so he could say a private prayer of his own to give him the words he would need for Hank.

"Klem, my friend, what did I do wrong in life that God is punishing me?"

"What?" answered Klem, "What could you ever mean by that question, Hank?"

"Klem, I have always been good with words when it comes to helping a customer decide whether to keep spending money for repairs on their old car or to trade it in on a newer one."

"Hank, you need not to try to balance your words for me, just take as long as you need and tell me what is troubling you."

Both Hank and Klem, sitting on the white oak bench, looked off into the sea as it played onto the rocky cliffs. Sometimes, the ocean shot upward turning the blue green saltwater into a beautiful fountain of white spray and foam fifteen or more feet high. It was quite a sight against the blue sky dotted with the ever-present seagulls.

Klem silently outlined the bench's wood grain with his finger. Hank mustered his words to tell Klem what was on his mind.

"Klem, I haven't told anyone else this. I mean, you are the first to know. Trish, my dear wife, may only have six months to live, so say the doctors in Port Smith. Lucky, for us, our son Tom has been able to keep the gas station going during Trish and my many trips to the oncology center. Klem, it really looks bad. It's a cancerous tumor somewhere near her stomach, and they think it may have spread. You know, Trish didn't want any chemo or radiation, but now she has taken the advice of the team of doctors and has resorted to medication for pain management."

"Gosh, Hank, I had no idea. I am so sorry this has happened!"

"Thanks, Klem. Trish is dealing with all this as well as any good, God-loving person could."

"Hank, is there anything I could do to help you? Really anything, you just name it."

"Well, as far as the day-to-day details of life, I think I have that covered. My business will be taken care of in my absence. It's just that I have this gnawing question in my spirit."

Klem looked at Hank, knowing that it was okay if some silence occurred between them and the park bench.

"Klem, sometimes I feel that I am questioning my faith, and that scares me a lot."

"Hank, my friend, faith is a journey. Just like a person taking a lifelong nature walk. Sometimes, your faith is strong, like you have reached the top of a hill in your walk. And sometimes, it is weak, like when you are in a valley. I call this my faith journey and everyone faces this in their lives. Hank, my friend, continue this walk and strive for the hilltop my friend."

"But how do I reach for that top when everything seems to be going wrong?"

"Well, my answer will seem so simple that it at first, it may feel like it can't be true, but it is. Hank, please don't stop praying. God wants to hear from us whether we are in the valley or on the hilltop. Remember miracles happen. Many times, miracles happen through the people here on Earth. These people may be doctors, pastors, or teachers. Or a miracle can happen through any of us too. Each and every one of us can be part of a miracle. We can pray for each other or with each other. Do you want to pray now together, Hank?"

Hank was listening carefully to his friend Klem, but kept his eyes focused on the vast sea horizon.

"Yes, please."

That night, Klem told his lovely wife that they had another family to put on their evening prayer list. Their prayer list was kept on their nightstand next to their bed. Sometimes, the names and their respective concerns were so numerous that this list was needed. They felt that God did not judge them when they needed a reminder of who they were going to pray for. Hank and his family were given sincere prayers to God by Klem and Jane every evening for many weeks to come.

Chapter 7

Nature Around Us

WITH SO MUCH NATURE AROUND him, Klem never felt alone. Today was Wednesday; "hump day" some call it. When hump day at work was finished, there were fewer days left before the weekend. Klem never felt a burden to work since becoming the lighthouse keeper. He knew, however, that he was truly lucky or blessed for that matter. Arriving at the base of his lighthouse, he leaned against it to catch his breath.

"I think I will walk around the base. Do an inspection tour, so to speak."

Once on the other side, the ocean side, the seagulls soared high in the blue sky.

"Seagulls," Klem thought in his mind, "beach scavengers. Some aligned them to rodents of the city, getting into fights over some rotten morsel."

Hundreds of mornings, Klem climbed to the lighthouse top just to do window cleaning. He had some clean rags and a bottle of Windex glass cleaner tucked in a small square box on the floor. Most of the window cleaning was due to seagull splatters. Once he finished that task, he went out to the railing to likewise freshen it. Many times, when gulls push off the railing to take into the sky, they deposit their white dropping on the iron work. The gulls are basically flat-footed but could stand on the wide circular brass railing that kept lighthouse keepers from stumbling off the narrow deck outside the lamphouse. It served as a grab rail so to speak. So, it was nice to keep it clean for himself as well as for the visitors who managed to complete the assent to the top.

Klem admired the seagulls even though their manners were kind of lacking. It was truly amazing how they could navigate the air currents, flying speed, and trajectory. Klem decided to take maybe a half hour this day, since the morning chores could wait at least that long. He needed some time with nature especially after learning about Hank's wife, Trish. He navigated down the rocks with his lunch box swinging slightly around his neck from a brown nylon rope. He planned to enjoy the beach and salt air for these next few minutes. During his little repast, Klem witnessed the most amazing sequence of natural mathematical application he ever saw.

A gull decided that it was time for breakfast and that a fresh cherrystone clam would do just fine. The gull spied just the ticket, a nicely sized clam next to some seaweed, both on the side of a partly submerged, crushed gray rockwall jetty. This jetty was only sometimes visible depending on the sea's wave action. The jetty was built by men previously out of work but then employed by the Public Works Administration of the 1930s after the stock market crashed, resulting in the Great Depression.

Just when the clam was above water, the gull landed next to it. The gull pulled and twisted the clam off from the wall after three attempts. With each try, the gull made sure that none of the other birds in the area were too close. Other gulls would quickly gather in a noisy crowd to steal his fresh meal.

Now that the industrious gull had the clam in her mouth, it was another thing to get it open. She flew the specimen down onto the beach where she rolled it around a bit and pecked at it. The clam was not going to open that easily. The gull looked at her clam and then peered around again to watch for any other of her kind that would take her harvest. At that point, the gull decided on another process to open the bivalve. With her strong sharp bill, she mouthed it and again took to the air.

Flying high over the cluster of rocks from which the mollusk was attached, the gull let her lunch drop at the precise trajectory. A forward momentum of fifteen miles an hour, and with the descent downward, the clam landed smack on top of the hard piece of granite rock. With a crack, the clam was split into five or more pieces. Soaring back around, she flew down to take the first taste of her fresh breakfast.

Admiring God's marvelous creation, Klem exclaimed, "Almighty God, you gave that seagull the first GPS system, way before man discovered your electricity!"

After that spectacle, throughout his lighthouse chores, Klem couldn't stop humming to himself some of his favorite hymns. A few hours later, Wednesday ended with yet another beautiful sunset. Klem gathered his lunch bag of empty Tupperware containers and headed down the dirt path back to his home. Jane would have some dinner starting soon; then, they would sit together on the couch and watch a few of their favorite television shows before going to bed. Who knows, he thought, maybe tonight would be root beer float night!

Chapter 8

Business as Usual

HANK ALWAYS WONDERED WHAT HIS day was going to be like at the gas station. He would never know what story or slice of life was going to come in through the door. Normally, his own life was that of running the gas station, helping customers, and keeping inventory on the shelves and storeroom.

Thursdays were no different from any other. He would arrive an hour before opening at 7:00 a.m. to pick up any UPS shipments that were left on the back cement porch. This morning, there were four boxes to open, inspect, and shelve or replenish the stockroom.

Today, Hank was working in slow motion, "Like moving in a sea of molasses" as his mother would say when he was a child. She would say that to young Hank when he had to clean his bedroom. Hank started to converse with himself in the quietness and solitude of his gas station.

Hank said to himself, "I'm just not into doing these things, at least not today. I think I'll make some herbal tea and just sit until nine o'clock."

Sometimes, when we are confronted with awful things in our lives like Trish's cancer, we realize just how powerless we are, and we can't change the outcome. So, during these awful times, we tend to reminisce about our past. Maybe it is a time when things were simpler with less worries.

Hank remembered one instance about twenty years ago when his house electrical fuse blew, leaving the furnace useless until he got another one at Burton's. It seemed the end of the world that day. It was hardly anything compared with what is happening in his life now.

Wouldn't you know, it decided to blow on the evening of his twin daughters's, Mary and Beth, high school prom. Up until now, and all day long, Trish excitingly took the girls to get their hair done, fingernails painted, and whatever else was "required"—all for the "never-to-be-forgotten" evening. Hank knew better than to interfere with "mother and daughter time," so he stayed away from all the prep-work. When the hour was right, as a loving father, he was to admire his daughters. This would not be hard to do since they would certainly look elegant.

Then, the darn house fuse had to pop just before the twins were deciding which one of them was going to shower first. To make things worse, the hot water heater was also on the same fuse circuit, something Burton told him a few times before to fix. Now, the house was getting colder, and the hot water was following the same fate, and the girls were starting to let their hormones take over. Surely, every lovely aspect of this event would be crushed, all because of their dad.

"Dad, you know I have to shower after running around all day. The house is freezing and the water is cold! Maybe Beth can, but I can't take a shower under these conditions! I think I'm just going to die! Die I tell you! My prom is ruined even before leaving the house! Dad, do something! Do anything!"

Hank knew he had about seven minutes to get to Burton's for a replacement fuse, that is, if he ran fast. See, there was no time to look for his misplaced car keys, another insurmountable dilemma. He knew better to keep this one problem only to himself. Hank got the fuse, went downstairs to the fuse box, replaced it, found his car keys, and just like magic. All was right with the world once again—yeah, a simpler life.

Chapter 9

An Adventure

FRIDAY, KLEM HEADED TO WORK, if you could call it "work," at the lighthouse. He liked it so much that it didn't seem like work. There were some things however that he did worry about. One day, sooner or later, the whole exterior would have to be whitewashed. Some of the stucco was starting to fail. In various places, little chunks would fall off, slowly sinking into the sea. Besides this worry, Klem was in turmoil with the news of Trish's tumor. He decided to climb the seventy-two steps as usual. Saying the Lord's prayer; and once on the top, he would deliver up his concern to God, feeling the warmth of the early rising sun as if it was God's own hand on his shoulders.

Friday, like all the days of the week, meant filling up the kerosene for the cloth wick to feed on. A daily task was pulling the vertical chains with their weights attached at the end to wind the rotating wick and concave mirror. The chains started at the lighthouse's base went all the way to the top and back down again. Like winding a grandfather's clock, this gave the wick the ability to rotate twenty-four hours a day within the Fresnel lens.

Forgoing his other duties of spray cleaning the lenses and tending the rose hips at the bottom, Klem left the lighthouse and hurried home to meet his son, Glenn. They had planned to take the short drive to one of Maine's lighthouses called "Manny Light" and do the tourist things that the visitors from the flatlands enjoyed over and over.

Glenn was a tall slender yet well-built youth having twenty-one years under his belt. He shared the love of the beach and the sea, but maybe for more of the adventure it could extend to him rather than Klem's total awe of God's finest creation. Even though they lived in the heart of the lobster harvest for the whole nation, Glenn preferred some meat that didn't come with a face and tail on his plate. That was probably his dad's fault. When Glenn was four years old, Klem bought him a red fuzzy stuffed lobster.

Glen was instantly delighted with the foot-long stuffed toy and made his dad have long conversations with it at bedtime. Glenn decided to call this little fluff just plain "Lobster." Lobster was this little boy's friend and was tucked under the blankets with him after they said their nighttime prayers.

Now as almost a full-grown man, Glenn still could not bring himself to order one of these creatures to be steamed alive and delivered on a plate.

"Dad, let's get a burger at that seasonal stand just off the road on the way to Manny Lighthouse and then an ice cream where they make their own."

Pat's Ice Cream Parlor had a reputation of costing a lot for their ice cream, but had a marketing ploy that worked as good as all the wonderful thirty-six flavors. Pat and her sister knew that if they made a "kiddy" sized cone using two generous scoops, their customers would talk about that "kiddy" size from time to time all summer long. The next size was called "small"—a three scooper—and then the next was a four scoop called "medium," followed by "large." It was five giant scoops towering from the cone. Customers would neglect that it cost a small fortune to delight a family of three or four kids. The thing they told their friends was, "You should see the size of their 'kiddy' cone not to mention their 'small' size!"

First-time customers to Pat's would gape at the size when the people in line received their dessert from the hand in the window. The workers inside, standing at an open window, would take your order and then close the window screen quickly to keep any flying insects from circling the drums of ice cream and the worker's heads. At night, bare yellow lights hung from several strands of black electrical wire overhead to keep most of the insects from the people waiting in line.

Glenn knew that his stomach was small, as flat as a washboard, but he wouldn't call it flat. Instead, he said that he was carrying a six pack, in reference to his stomach muscles. Klem thought it was funny when Glenn would also say, "Dad, it's time for my two-hour feeding! Good thing we have arrived at Pat's Ice Cream just in time."

It was funny, but it was even more true than funny. The kid needed something to eat eight or more times a day. After ordering their cones, they decided to eat the ice cream at the same time, while driving to Manny Light.

Manny Light was a proud lighthouse; again, like so many, it was perched on granite cliffs high above a boiling crashing turbulent sea. At one time, when society did less with material blessings, for a mere twenty-five cents, you could use a metal viewer that was attached to a metal pole stand. It was a pair of binoculars, and the quarter would give the customer about three minutes of use. After these three minutes, an internal shield would fall over the lenses making it darker than the inside of a cow. There was a lower perch of tubular metal that the shorter kids could stand on to help align their faces into the metallic optics, which was quite a marvel. The last one was taken away twelve years ago, probably sold for metal scrap or, if lucky, donated to a museum. Now, every household would have several pairs of binoculars, probably at least one pair for every member of the family.

Klem and Glenn found a parking spot just as another car was pulling out. Once outside, the two took off to the fence to view the lighthouse and cliffs. Running ahead of his dad, Glenn paused just for a moment and yelled, "Hey, Dad! Let's go around the fence for a better look!"

With that Glenn, maneuvered through an opening in the chain-linked fence. Klem saw that the fence also held a warning to stay on the parking lot side, but it seemed that his years melted away in those few seconds, and Klem was his own son's buddy on a kind of fantasy trip.

For years, starting from his first sight of the lighthouse as a toddler, this was just what he wanted to do. Later in life, the impulse never left him, but he couldn't bring himself to be this dangerously naughty. Now, like a child, Klem galloped along after his son, figuring Glenn would very soon stop at any time.

"Dad! Look at that rocky ledge down there. It's just like a wonderful staircase that probably goes clear around the lighthouse!"

Once on the narrow rock "staircase," Manny Light was thirty or more feet above them, and the ocean was about fifty feet below. This narrow cut in the cliff where the two were adventuring continued in front of them; however, it constantly led only to the left.

With excited breath of his youth, Glenn announced to his dad, "I bet we could go totally around the lighthouse just by finding our way on this rock ledge."

The rock ledge was totally naturally made. It wasn't meant to be traveled by. The ledge went from about three feet wide to about two measly feet wide. To make things worse, the narrow cliff ledge stopped completely right in front of Glenn. Klem was behind his son by about five feet.

"Dad, to continue on, we have to jump this channel. But it won't be too hard. It's not that wide. We will be able to jump across it in midair." Of course, before any more level-headed planning could occur, Glenn jumped across leaving Klem on the other side. Fifty feet below Klem's own feet was the churning white ocean surf with the tide quickly coming in. The sound of the water crashing into and out of the narrow channel would normally be pleasant to Klem, but now, it was seemingly warning "Why are you here?"

"Dad, come on. Come on!"

The channel was only the three feet across, and Klem certainly couldn't leave his son alone on the other side, especially with the tide rapidly rising in giant pulses. Tons of saltwater would soon reach up to pull them into the submerged rocks even further below.

Glenn still did not seem to grasp the total danger of their situation. This was real life, not like a safe a dream ride in Disney World where nothing could possibly hurt you. This was truly life-threatening. The jump was made—more like a giant skip—and on the other side, Glenn was there to steady his dad's forward momentum. Klem's heart was pounding so violently that he could feel his pulse clear into his jaw. A few moments later, he saw his son reach for something stuck in the wall side of the cliff.

"Dad, look, a seagull feather!"

And with that proclamation, Glenn pulled the single feather from a slit in the rock and let it go into the wind. Klem's life was fading as he watched the feather take its flight down…down…down to be swallowed up by the ocean water a half a minute later. Klem wondered what the local newspaper would write about them, if the coast guard ever found their bodies.

By this point, the ledge was only a few inches wider than a foot, too dangerous to make the maneuver needed to turn around to go back. The only way was forward, an uncertain path. Klem and Glenn took one turn left, one after another, going slower and slower as the wet rock ledge became even narrower. Again, the ledge continued to curve around to the left. Glenn's body was partially hidden from Klem's view even though Glenn was only five or so feet in front of his dad.

Fifteen minutes passed, inching along, Klem dared not to look down. He tasted the saltwater spray on his lips coming from way below their feet. At this point, Glenn stopped inching forward. Oh my God, Klem thought, I hope he wasn't frozen with fright, or just as bad, was he stopping because there was no more place to go except to our death?

On Glenn's left, he found a flat spot on the cliff side just above his shoulders. They had been traveling up ever so slightly as they inched forward, and now this flat spot was the top of the cliff. Green grass and wild flowers were growing in the sunlight. So close, yet so far, the top was at Glenn's shoulder height. Glenn could just see it over the cliff wall where he was clinging. Klem had no idea what Glenn was going to do with this discovery. One thing's for sure—they've reached the very end of the narrow ledge. Klem then witnessed something with total disbelief of his own eyes. With one powerful twist toward the cliff and upward, Glenn swung his entire body up high and onto the grassy top. A split second later, Klem saw his son's hand reaching down to him.

"Dad, grab my hand. I'll pull you up."

Klem knew that this either would save his life or, with his own weight, would pull both of them down forty feet onto the rocky, frothing saltwater to their demise. Again and again, by the force of the crashing ocean, their bodies would be cut to ribbons against the powerful rocks.

Klem thought, "Could I risk my son to save myself?"

Above Klem's head, once again, Glenn yelled, "Dad, grab my hand. I'm reaching down! See my hand? I'll pull you up!"

To keep from flipping when grabbing for his dad, Glenn knew he had to lay flat on his stomach. He made his sneaker-clad feet spread way apart to make a human triangle for stabilization. With the adrenalin God gives at these times, Klem responded to his son's command. With one quick motion, Glenn reached down, grabbed his dad's hand, and swung him up into the air and onto the flatland.

They lay there among the grasses for a few minutes feeling the sun on their faces.

"Thank you, God. Thank you, Glenn," Klem said feebly with his heart still pounding.

They both knew this was truly the stupidest thing either one of them had ever done, or even dreamed of.

After gaining their earthly composure, both father and son rose to their feet. Off in the distance, they could see tourists with their binoculars plastered to their faces focusing on both of them. Others were pointing this way and that to direct other tourists to the scene, but not one of them venturing past the warning sign—the very sign Glenn and Klem slipped past a little less than an hour ago.

The car trip home was a little quiet and pensive. The only stop was at Pat's Ice Cream; both requested a kiddy size ice cream cone of "rocky road." Klem thought that that name of ice cream flavor was rather appropriate, considering what they just experienced. "Heavenly help" would have been a better name.

With their ice cream cones in hand, Klem and Glenn went back into Klem's parked car. Seated in the front, both guys just stared ahead through the windshield for a while without moving very much.

"Dad, what are we going to tell Mom about our day?"

After a few more licks of ice cream, in an attempt to manicure the few drips on the side of his cone, Klem responded, "Mom probably knows about it already. She has that second sense. Over our thirty-five years of marriage, mind you, God blessed me each of those days. Your mom? Somehow, more times than not, she knows what I have done, sometimes even before I did it or, for that matter, *even before I thought about doing any darn thing!*"

This strange realization broke the intensity, making both of the adventurers light-hearted once again.

Klem continued, "In the rare case that she doesn't know, let's just tell her... uhm, well we will start out with... uhm... Glenn, my dear son, maybe she will have gone to bed by the time we get home."

Chapter 10

Gifts

FROM TIME TO TIME, TOWNSPEOPLE as well as "out-of-towners" visited Gray Cliff Lighthouse, bearing an assortment of nautical gifts. Klem would always and graciously accept them no matter the condition or the nature of the gift. He always enjoyed the wooden lobster floats that people would leave. Each wooden float was painted in bright colors and different patterns. The patterns and colors painted on the floats were unique to each lobsterman who harvested the area waters. These bobbing floats on the ocean surface were attached by a rope to a lobster trap resting on the ocean floor.

Lobster traps were wooden cages with a funnel of woven rope inside. The older cages had rope made of twisted strands of hemp, while the newer ones used nylon rope. Once the trap was placed in the ocean, if a lobster ventured inside to get some yummy bait, it couldn't find its way out. The rope funnel was basically a one-way path. It is illegal for anyone but the trap owner to harvest from it. Just as important, it was also against their strict code of ethics for any lobsterman to pull a trap and take its catch from any float that was not theirs. After a while, some floats would break away from its tethered rope, worn thin by the constant movement of the ocean. Especially after a storm, the floats could be found washed up on the beach.

When Klem found a float on the beach, he would nail the float on the side of the picket fence that outlined the perimeter of the land surrounding the light. He had a collection of at least fifty-two lobster floats in total. Most of the recent, donated ones, were purchased from souvenir-type stores, but Klem didn't mind.

One very unexpected gift came from Slim Newcome, a visitor from New Jersey. Totally unannounced beforehand, Slim trucked a sixteen-foot rowboat all that way, delivering it to Klem's lighthouse site. Slim was so proud to present his gift, and without a doubt, it was noble. Before leaving however, Slim asked for a donation slip for tax purposes.

Klem said, "Well, Slim, no one asked me for a donation slip before, but I can write something on my letterhead paper from the lighthouse museum."

Slim said, "Well, if it isn't too much for me to ask you to do, I would appreciate it."

The rowboat's framing was prebent oak, and the floor timbers were likewise oak. During its construction, each five-inch outside hull boards were placed so that they overlapped the previous one for the boat to take shape. The boards were fashioned to the inside curved ribbing by copper nails hammered by hand. Any copper nail that did not pierce into the ribbing was bent at the end so it would not work itself out. Before placing each board, they were softened in a steaming case and held to the correct bend. Without steaming, the boards would fight the curve or split all together.

Klem had entirely no idea what donation price he should state on his little note. Many years ago, this rowboat was a fine little well-built vessel. At this stage of its life, the poor thing was pretty well beat.

Klem was not an expert in boats, but knew that each overlapping board made a ledge that pulled and trapped air bubbles when the boat went forward. In a small way, the trapped air bubbles made the boat weigh less when the boat traveled faster. He also knew that the boards would swell enough so that any opening between the wood components would eventually seal shut and the hull would be water tight.

Klem came back with his little note that Slim asked for. "Well, Slim, why don't you just research it yourself and put what you think is a fair price to use as a tax deduction."

Slim thought that was just fine, as he turned his rig around the small parking area. Continuing down the hill, he waved back at Klem warmly, and then he was gone. On Slim's way home, he smiled, feeling that both benefited by his trip and that he had done a marvelous deed.

Klem looked at his new gift and said, "Well, God, maybe I can make a planter out of this poor thing or maybe I'll just keep it here by the gift shop's stone walkway. It may add some character somehow."

God didn't answer him right away, so Klem thought God was in agreement that maybe it would make some character or build some character, somehow.

Chapter 11

God Is with Us

Hours turned into days, which turned into weeks, Klem and Jane would talk with Hank after church, but Hank seemed to want to visit Klem at the lighthouse again.

"Klem, do you think I can talk with you again at the bench? How about tomorrow?"

He really didn't give Klem any time to think about it and risk a "no" answer. Klem would not have blown off a visit from Hank, and he was hoping that maybe some good news might be on the horizon with Trish, just maybe.

"Sure, Hank. I'll be mowing with the push mower at the lighthouse starting 8:30 a.m. It is not a lot of acreage. See you then."

That Monday, Klem fetched his work gloves and the push mower from a small shed and started on the grass. The little lawn around the lighthouse and the original lighthouse keeper's attached house was so small that the grass cutting didn't even bring about any perspiration on his forehead. Besides, it was a soothing task since there was no gasoline engine smells or noise. It fitted in quite well with the inspiration of the bluff and the light.

Klem saw his friend Hank coming up the hill from where the parking lot for six or seven car spaces was located. He gave the lawn mower one last push to finish the row and turned to meet Hank on their bench.

So here sat two friends, Klem and Hank, Hank being the first to speak. Klem had a good idea what his question for him would be, since he himself, had been plagued with Hank's concerns for several months now.

"Klem, I really need to know... why did this happen to me and Trish? I mean, we have been good Lutherans, going to church every Sunday, raising Tom, Mary, and Beth to know our Lord, and volunteering in so many projects around the church. You know how I have reopened my gas station after hours for any repairs Pastor Dell needed on the little church school bus. The church board of trustees could always trust me to repair or maintain the bus correctly. I never charged the church for anything, for either parts or my labor. Why did God do this to me?"

Over the years, Klem had wrestled with this kind of question many times. Sometimes, it would just kind of get into his brain again, usually when he was sitting inside the lamphouse of the lighthouse high above the rock-filled beach below. Klem felt closer to God way up there. He could almost feel the breath of God in the wind as it swirled in from the open hatch that lead to the outside circular walk-way and railing.

Nothing really answered Klem directly such as a Godly voice from the clouds, like it happened in the Old Testament. After much prayer, which is just talking to God, Klem just seemed to get his answer.

"Hank, my dear friend, let me tell you what I believe. Now, this is just my belief. It may not be Protestant, Catholic, or Jewish. But it is just what I believe my God has told me."

Hank prepared himself, shifting his weight on the hard bench a little and wiping some moisture from his swollen eyes.

"See, both good and bad things happen to all of us. It is the downfall of the Garden of Eden where only good things happened all the time. Adam and Eve, the first man and woman, decided to commit the first sin against God. This allowed the devil and bad things to get mixed with God's pure world. God does not want bad things to happen, but they do. If it is God who makes bad things to happen, why would He let it happen to His followers? If this was true, He would only allow terrible things to happen to bad people to punish them. Only His followers would be given a lovely life, filled with a bowl full of cherries.

This would also prove the existence of God. The good would always be rewarded, and the bad would be punished each and every time. See Hank, good and bad things happen to both good and bad people. It just happens, since Adam and Eve were sent out of Eden."

Hank searched for some comfort in Klem's words and allowed him to continue.

"Furthermore, I believe our Heavenly Father hurts inside when he sees injustice happening to His creation. God created man in his own image. Not that God has a body with arms and legs like us, but that the image He spoke of is that of feeling both happiness and awful mental pain. When something happens down here on Earth that is truly a caring loving act from one human to another, God feels happiness. Conversely, when something happens such as a death of a newborn child or a murder, God hurts terribly inside. See, my friend, God does not make a murder or a child's death occur to teach us a lesson or to bring us closer to Him. No, not my God. It just happens, Hank. It just happens.

Now, this is the important point, our God, our heavenly Father, has promised no matter what happens, He will be with you until your last breath of life. It could be in a hospital room with life-support-ing tubes and medical machinery all around you. It could be with a young service woman or man in a dark cold prison camp. Things may not get better in that hospital room nor would someone be rescued from a prison camp. Even more important, however, God is with you, around you—in you. No matter where, He will be with us all.

Hank, He is with you in your gas station, He is here sitting on this very bench with us, or in Trish's hospital room. I know this is my comfort because there is nothing more important anywhere than my God. And I know that He will be with me, you, Trish, and all believers. He is with us all the way to that perfect shining light, light of perfect health and perfect love in heaven. And that will be forever."

Hank reached for his cloth hanky from his pocket to blot the healing tears from his eyes, but it was his soul that was healing. Klem was right—our God will be with us not just when we need Him, but every moment of our lives, not to bring a perfect life for us, but for all of us to be His very own children.

"Hank, this is the time we must remember to have a childlike faith. Try not to dive into the whys and how's, but just have a faith like a child, unquestioning. Our answers will be revealed to us not in this life but in our next, in heaven. But when we finally arrive in heaven, maybe these earthly questions will not be nagging for answers. And Hank, you must know that Jane and I haven't stopped praying for Trish, and you must not either. Pray for Trish and pray for yourself too, Hank."

"Thanks, Klem, you are a good friend."

Hank got to his feet and hugged Klem awkwardly but with Christian love. He paused a few more moments to see his friend's face. The gleaming salt-sprayed stucco lighthouse was now bathing the two in a light shadow. With only silence speaking, Hank shook Klem's hand and parted having felt that he had receive a vision of God's love from that old gentleman.

Klem hoped that his words and his belief would help Hank especially at this time with his beloved Trish's declining health.

Chapter 12

Village Life

ON SATURDAY MORNING, ON AUGUST 15, Klem was doing his "inspection tour" as he jokingly called it when he walked around the outside of his modest Victorian house. Nearly all of Jane's flowers were in full bloom, with the rose hips taking over, a little more than he expected. Sidewalk repair was in full swing, as the wooden forms would soon be filled with concrete. The pothole outside the IGA was filled properly with asphalt back in May.

During one of the village meetings, it was brought to vote whether or not to keep the black iron antique street lamps or replace them with modern and more efficient sodium-vapor lights. It was a close vote; but for the next five years, the old street lamps were to light the way; after then, another vote would be needed.

On every fourth block within the village, there were mailboxes that would "magically" receive stamped envelopes, and a few days later, the mail would arrive at the correct address. Whenever Klem mailed his letters and bills, he would check the time of pickup, not that it ever changed, but it was habit. After opening the mailbox door, placing the letters on top, and closing the metal flap, Klem would open the door one more time to make sure the letters fell safely into the belly of the mailbox. In the sixty-five years of his life, never did a piece of mail get stuck on the mailbox flap, but he had to check it anyway, maybe a habit.

"Nothing wrong with that!" Klem would say under his breath as he looked to the sky for any possibility of rain even if it was clear and sunny.

The little houses in the Port James although small are laced with wonderful character. Each home had shutters at the windows; Klem's were hunter green and had hand cutouts of a lighthouse on each. With many of the homes, the original rain gutters were made of wood. No one in the village felt it was right to change them out to aluminum or vinyl even though that would require less maintenance. Walking down the village streets, every few years, one could see the Watercrests, the Chases, the Whitestones, the Jingles, or any of the other neighbors meticulously scraping, priming, and repainting various details of their homes.

The front yards were only fifteen or less feet from the sidewalk, and it seemed that everyone knew each other. Klem's living room was located in the front of his home, which during the summer months afforded him and his neighbors pleasantries as they walked passed.

Any number of neighbors out for a Sunday stroll or walking their dogs could see Klem inside or, on a nice day, sitting outside on his front steps or lawn.

"Hi, Klem," they would greet him, "Good morning. How's the family?" Tokens of verbal exchange that really meant, "Hey, don't forget. We love you!"

Klem would respond in likewise manner delivering the same message and feelings to each neighbor.

Sometimes, Klem brought his breakfast into his front room or even outside, especially when one of the village festivals occurred. It really wasn't the festival that brought him out onto a folding lawn chair right by the sidewalk; rather, it was the 5K run that was part of the festivities. Maybe it was Klem's subtle New England humor, but he felt a little smile grow across his face when the runners jogged by. The runners were all full of sweat and puffing, and their legs and feet pulsed with agony. Klem would acknowledge each jogger by lifting up his fork speared with a nice plump breakfast sausage or a fold of buckwheat pancake. Of course, his pancakes dripped with real maple syrup and farm fresh butter. Not that it needed, but during this morning run, his hot breakfast seemed to "go down the hatch" even easier.

Caught between not being cute little boys anymore but not old enough to place in the 5K run were the Cooper boys, Link and Jake, twins in fact of twelve years. Mr. and Mrs. Cooper was a good-natured village couple—one of those kinds of families who could be traced back at least four generations living within the same village. In fact, the Coopers were living in the house that Mr. Cooper grew up in; his parents now deceased. The home was not really ailing but kept Burton and his hardware business on the receiving end of plumbing, electrical, and general house repair questions.

Chapter 13

The Cooper Boys and Some Chicken

SOME TWINS ARE DRESSED THE same by their parents, but Mrs. Cooper never went that route with them, even as babies. She did however preferred bold horizontal stripes. Since she managed the cloth purchasing for the family, her boys always wore collarless striped shirts. It seemed that collars were just another thing to get dirty, so why pay more for a shirt with collars?

Her boys, Link and Jake, always traveled together, all the time. If they were buying a doughnut in Janet's Bakery and if Link had to go to the firehouse where there was a bathroom, Jake would find himself feeling the pressure inside his body as well. Neither of them viewed crosswalks as something they needed to use. Without ever saying, they both decided it was too much bother to walk twenty more steps to crosswalk.

They were not bad boys. They were full of that great enthusiasm that sometimes disappears when we reach forty or so. No matter what the subject was, the boys had tons of energy to tell their stories. Catching a friendly eye from some polite adult they knew, the Cooper boys exhausted their audience recounting some adventure. It didn't matter where they met anyone. It could be right in the middle of the street or at the checkout line in the IGA. Telling some incredible story, they usually tired out their polite audience.

Their parents soon learned that with the boy's birthdays and Christmas, every present had better be purchased and wrapped in duplicate. If it was time for their first wristwatch, of course both had to have one, likewise with their first real two-wheeled bicycle. To avoid any possible hassle on Christmas morning, Mr. and Mrs. Cooper bought two identical bicycles, even down to the same color, red. Red was neither of the boy's favorite color, but this way the boys wouldn't fight over either color, kind of leveling the playing field.

Nine months ago, when Christmas morning came, the bicycles were wrapped the best they could have been. The night before Christmas however, Mr. Cooper took the bicycles out of their boxes. To his dismay, he had quite an assortment of nuts, bolts, and other unknown bicycle parts that flowed out of the box and piled squarely into his lap.

Mr. Cooper talked to himself saying to the shiny pile of parts, "You sure don't look like a bicycle."

So, it was a late Christmas evening before Mr. Cooper finished the job.

"I should be in bed with my nightcap on and dreaming of sugar plums dancing in my head or however that poem goes."

So by Christmas morning, each bike flanked the brick fireplace, Jake's on the left and Link's on the right. The Christmas tree stood in the bay window that looked over blue white snow—the color you can only see in the early morning or early evening. Link and Jake felt that they must be in heaven since they were hinting for their first new bikes for three months before Christmas, "nonstop" as Mr. and Mrs. Cooper would say.

Another winter faded into history and then spring gave new birth again. Summer eventually took hold, the lazy, crazy days of summer. Summer meant lots of bike riding and with the Cooper boys, with their bikes almost became part of their human anatomy.

Whenever they went into town or a little beyond, the shiny red bikes would transport them under one "boy power" each. Link and Jake loved to take a picnic lunch and sit along the canal, which was built through the center of Port James. In many ways, it is a beautiful piece of engineering. It was constructed in the early 1800's by immigrants from Ireland, where the potato crop had failed too many times. The men only needed to have strong backs and able to work for long twelve-hour days. One mission of the canal was to transport grain to the flour mills in the city. On average, the canal is seventy-five feet wide and twelve feet deep and boasts a 236-mile length. It passes through many small towns on its way to the coastal cities. Once transported and delivered by flat barges, the grain was taken off by hand in fifty-pound sacks to the mills for processing. It is not used today except for pleasure craft.

Over 200 years ago, along one side of the canal, there is a path where the harnessed oxen pulled the barges with ropes as they walked with their team leader.

Today, these oxen paths are shaded with beautiful mature willow and maple trees and wild flowers. Couples and families bike or stroll along these paths, sometimes visiting several hamlets and villages along the way. Toward evening, the lights from the village, and if lucky the moon, are reflected in the canal's water surface. The mirror like reflection is periodically interrupted by the paddling of mallard duck families looking to nibble freshwater weeds along the banks. Sometimes, the canal banks of earth and rock are ten feet high, and other times, they are almost nonexistent, only a few feet below the nearby landscape. Several places throughout the length are mechanical locks that can raise or lower water levels within the lock. This allows vessels to travel along different elevations.

Five years ago, during a Port James village meeting, the residents voted to build a small park with a white gazebo overlooking the canal. The Fire Department donated the land that is called "Fireman's Field." Each Wednesday evening of summer, various musical groups use the gazebo stage to entertain villagers. Concerts start at 7:00 p.m. and lasts for two hours. An hour before each concert, Ellen Palmer sets up her food truck selling hotdogs, hamburgers, chicken sandwiches, chips, and soda.

Just past this park is the lift bridge crossing over the canal. This bridge boasts of sparkling blue paint, the state color. It is lit at night with nautical lamps that are softly captured by the reflection in the water. The lift bridge is tended by a state employee who sits either in a small house or in a wooden tower right near the bridge. When this bridge tender receives a call that a boat is nearing, he hits the levers, stopping the traffic on Union Street, and slowly raises the bridge.

The bridge does not tilt one way or another, but totally rises above the canal like a metal road twenty-five feet high. On either entrance of the bridge are open air metal staircases, where pedestrians can take the metal steps and cross over while the bridge is in the raised position. When walking on the bridge in the "up" position, boats navigating the canal can be seen traveling under one's feet.

This marvel was another source of fun for the brothers, Link and Jake. When the bridge was going up, the cross gates would lower, stopping traffic. Bells ring their warning and the red lights flash. Of course, Link and Jake would come biking as fast as they could when they heard the warning bells as if they were ringing for them to come. It was fun to watch the ascent of the bridge while the watercraft passed under. Sometimes when the state canal tugboat went through, Link and Jake would strain their neck to look inside the tug's windows and hope for a wave from the captain.

As boys would do, both argued with each other as to which one would land a tugboat captain's job. The teasing would usually end with some good-natured pushing between them. This jostling was just enough to throw the other off balance from their bicycle seats while they kept one leg stretched down to the pavement for balance.

During one of these bridge performances, Link came up with what he thought was a unique "I dare you" game.

"Hey, Jake, I want to play chicken with you, if you dare."

Even though Jake had no vision of what Link was daring, he had to keep up his twelve-year-old honor and replied, "I can do anything you can do, Link. I'm not chicken!"

"Oh, yes, you are Jake. Chicken! Chicken! Chicken! Cluck! Cluck! Cluck!" This of course was accompanied with the necessary arm gestures of a silly-looking flapping chicken.

"All right, enough! What is your dare, Link? You silly bird!"

With a little push of his foot on the road, Link gained his balance on this bike and stopped right next to the lift bridge, which was just starting its trip down back onto the pavement. Link dismounted and placed his bike's front tire right in the way where the bridge could descend directly onto.

"What are you doing, Link?" Jake asked in astonishment, "If you don't move your bike wheel, it's going to be crushed by the bridge!"

Link retorted in a jeering, gleeful way, "See, you are chicken! Put your front wheel next to mine, whoever pulls their wheel out first is chicken."

By now, Jake had enough, "For crying out loud in a bucket, Link, I'll do it too. I'm not a chicken!"

It was only a little more than thirty seconds before the slowly descending bridge might claim at least one of their wheels.

"Remember Jake, this is the dare, or should I call you chicken-Jake? Don't be the first one to pull back your wheel! Cluck! Cluck! Cluck!"

This was just too much for Jake, and with blood pressure mounting, he promised to himself he would show his brother, at any cost.

The bridge got closer and closer to the pavement and equally closer to the two front wheels of their bikes. Neither one budged to pull away their bike to safety. Then, it happened, inches away Link pulled away and Jake was the winner, but for only a fraction of a second. His poor new Christmas bike wheel was feeling the pressure of the descending bridge. With utterly no match, Jake's tire was being crushed before his very eyes. With squeals of terror, Jake yanked it out only to see his poorly bent wheel with the shiny chrome spokes torn away and pointing in an array of many directions.

Coming from only the way a loving brother could, Link fell off his bike and started to roll around right on the cement sidewalk laughing and laughing so much that he could hardly get the words out.

"You silly goose, look at your wheel! Dad and Mom are going to get you now!"

It was bad enough to lose the wheel of his bike, but now Jake would have to face his parents. He already knew that to defend why he had to do this was not the tactic to start with. It sounded so silly, and his parents would certainly lead with that exact point. All the way home, Link still had thousands of muffled giggles that just couldn't be kept in. It was so funny to see Jake's front bike wheel try to turn, but instead, it wobbled uselessly in one place as his brother limped the pitiful thing along.

When they got home, Jake decided to ease into the whole story slowly. He would leave his shambled bike propped against the house in the back, next to the kitchen screen door. Like a new recruit in the U.S. Army, he proceeded up the wooden steps into the kitchen to meet his parents. Mr. and Mrs. Cooper were having their midafternoon coffee, seated at the kitchen table. There was a paper flier on the dinette table, which they were both reading between sips of their drink. They were discussing whether or not to vote on the central school budget. It was only a three-percent increase over last year, so they both felt they would do their duty and vote "yes." The voting always took place in the Lutheran Church basement. The voting was the next day; but unknown to them, another decision had to be made even sooner, a domestic one.

It really didn't take either parent very long to sense something wrong with Jake. The first hint was that Link was not with him. Link knew he would make things worse by his uncontrollable giggles, even though he did feel a little sorry for Jake.

Link stayed outside in the sun and tried to listen through the screen door to assess his brother's progress, but he could only hear muffled tones coming from the family trio.

After what seemed like fifteen minutes, Mrs. Cooper opened the door and motioned Link to come inside. Mr. Cooper lined the two boys up next to the kitchen shelves so both parents could look at each boy's expressions. They said nothing but just eyed both brothers from their table. Sometimes, the silence was the hardest punishment—the look of disappointment on their parent's faces was cutting into both boys's souls.

Finally, the judgment was presented. Mr. Cooper speaking for him and his wife, saying, "Boys, as you know, we are disappointed in both of you. Link, for pulling your brother into this silly game, and Jake, for going along with it. So, you are both equally in the wrong. As you know, the village festival is this week, which means the opening parade, carnival rides, cotton candy, and games of chance. Your mom and I were going to give both of you twenty dollars each to spend, but each of your twenty dollars will be used to pay for Jake's replacement wheel and tire. Even if Mr. Tucker at his hardware store ordered your wheel and tire, it will take over a month to arrive. As further punishment Link, you may not use your bike until your brother's is fixed. Now, go outside and sit on the front stairs until I tell you that you can go."

Somehow, stairs were a place where growing boys could decide what to do or where to go on a Saturday or any day during the summer. It was also a place where they could evaluate their actions, good or bad. Later on, it would be a place where a boy of teenage years could strike an impressive pose leaning on the post hoping a flock of girls from up the streets would slow down to admire how much he had matured over the summer.

Chapter 14

Entrepreneurs

SINCE BOTH BROTHERS WERE NOW without wheels for fun and transportation, some other element had to fill their summer emptiness. On Monday, Tuesday, or Wednesday, Jake and Link really didn't know what day it was since it was three months of summer vacation and every day seemed like a Saturday. Maybe a brother versus brother computer game competition, called "Escape from Wild Mountain," would fit the bill for them.

It happened to be Wednesday, and Mrs. Cooper was getting together the plants for the church sale. She had a fine talent of raising a whole variety of plant species that proliferated outside her home. The brick walkway absorbed the Maine spring sun, transferring its heat to the soil and then to the flower roots. Early in the growing season, this gave the tulips and daffodils a little head start. She didn't know why they germinated so nicely, but she just decided it was God's way of making sure there were flowers on the altar every Sunday. Mrs. Cooper supplied the altar flowers each Sunday in the summer as well as for the upcoming church sale.

Just at the right time, she would capture the seeds and grew them in starter pots; they would be nice hearty plants by time of the sale. Some might say that Mrs. Cooper single-handedly was the one source of flowers for her whole church. Her dining room bay window was the perfect place for this nursery of little green sprouts.

"Boys!" she announced from the dining room with hands on her hips, "You better not be in that living room in front of that game again on such a beautiful God-given day like today." And without waiting for an answer, she said, "Now scoot. Play outside until it is time for lunch!"

And so, with that, the Cooper brothers put away their game controls and took to the front door. Sitting on the steps, both elbows on their knees and hands cupping their faces, the thought process of two twelve year olds was sent into motion.

After some silent thought and squashing some carpenter ants that were zigzagging around in what seemed like pointless effort, Link said, "I got it! Why don't we see if old man Klem needs any work done at the lighthouse! Maybe he will give us some money that we can use for ice cream or battery-operated horns for our bikes!

Jake thought that was a great idea, thinking about having both a new wheel and a horn.

"Oh," jeered Link, "I forgot you only have half a bike!"

"Yeah, Link, but think, when all is said and done, my bike will be newer than yours, at least in the front!"

With that, they performed the traditional and required brother-pushing-brother walk, trying to knock each other off balance.

So, off the duo walked to check out their prospects, all the while kicking stones in front of them, dirt flying in the sunlight. The Gray Cliff Lighthouse was not too far away, up a hill from town. Passing through the parking spots, both boys pretended the white parking lines were tight ropes where they needed to keep their balance to stay on. Arms outstretched to keep balanced, soon they were at the steps of the lighthouse gift shop. Klem was inside, taking inventory with a little notebook of green-lined paper and pen to check what little treasures he should restock.

One popular item in the gift shop was a little blue lighthouse passbook. After visiting Port James lighthouse and any other lighthouses, visitors could get the lighthouse gift shop clerk to stamp it with their own special outline of the lighthouse they just climbed.

It cost fifty cents to stamp the "passbook." When the passbook was filled, it could be mailed to an address on the back for a congratulation document. The passbook would be returned along with a handsome document a few weeks later. Klem noted that he may need to get another ink pad since this one was in the gift shop was wearing out.

Another article in the gift shop was multicolored nylon welcome mats. The wholesaler explained to Klem that these mats are made of used nylon cords from lobster traps. Instead of cutting the traps loose in the sea after their usefulness was over, the cords and traps were remade into these mats. This way, any variety of sea creatures would not mistake the nylon cords for prey and have it end up in their stomachs, possibly killing them.

"Hi, Mr. Watercrest," said the boys with enthusiastic unison.

"Top of the morning to you, my good young men. What brings you here this fine morning?" Klem put on an Irish brogue, which both boys took in stride even though it was not his normal way of talking.

Link spoke for the both of them, "We were just wondering if you had any work for us to do around here." Link added, "Yea, you know for money." He figured that it would be best to get this straight right from the beginning.

"Oh, I see," said Klem looking at Caroline Frome, the fifth-grade teacher who worked during the summer months at the gift shop. She liked volunteering since the old light housekeeper's home, now the gift shop, had so many windows to look out every direction. It was like being outside. If time permitted, she also liked swapping stories with Klem about the customers after they left. She was always amazed by the great distance vacationers would travel to visit the coast. Then too, it was so wonderful to be living in the very places that others could just cherish for a few vacation days at best.

"Caroline, can you think of any paying jobs these two fine lads could perform to stay out of trouble... ur, I mean... to make this place even more pleasant?"

"Well, Mr. Watercrest, we could use some boys to whitewash the picket fence that separates the parking lot from the south side lawn. The ocean breeze, especially toward that direction, plays havoc on those painted slats."

Klem though for a moment. In his head, he could envision the two boys fighting over the bucket of paint instead of taking turns dipping their paint brushes. His vision continued with the boys trying, with total innocent expressions on their faces, to explain to Klem or Caroline why the paint was spilled all over the parking lot. It would remain one of those great mysteries how footprints of white paint on the nice brick walkway could be seen all the way up from the fence, through the parking lot, and then up to the gift shop steps.

"Uhmm, let me think, Caroline."

He looked at the Cooper boys. They return Klem's calculating gaze with the most pleading Labrador puppy dog eyes he had ever seen.

"Maybe you could pull the weeds that have ventured into the small gardens around the lighthouse. Just stay away from the rose hips, we don't want you two coming back with thorns for me to have to take out of your hands."

"Now, boys," continued Klem, "let us settle on an hourly pay for you both."

Link piped in without a moment's hesitation, "I was thinking of fifty dollars an hour for each of us."

Klem, keeping back a little chuckle, replied, "How about fifty cents an hour for each of you?"

"Yeah!" said Link. "It's a deal. It's a deal!"

Both twins, excited as ever, were cheering and running around in a circle as if chasing each other, with hands waving and fingers wiggling, a regular three-ring circus. Klem looked at the two of them clad in their T-shirts, stripes going around their chest and waists doing their victory dance. He thought they looked much like honeybees in their beehive. After these festivities were done, Klem showed the duo the basement under the gift shop where they would find their garden tools and gloves.

Once Klem came back inside, Caroline said, "Well, Mr. Klem, you made them pretty happy!"

"Yes, they are pretty good kids, really. I'm sure however that after a few days, they will find something else to occupy their time."

Things grew fast in the Maine summer months. They had to since the growing season was only about four months long. Sunshine was plentiful, but rain came frequently enough to keep everything nourished. The fact is, once Link and Jake would finish weeding each garden on the grounds of the lighthouse, four in all, and weeding around the lighthouse itself, Klem was thinking ahead a little. He thought if things went well, the boys could weed both sides of the white picket fence around the parking lot.

Each day, the twins reported for work, about thirty minutes later than the day before. Klem however gave them credit for coming at all. It was cute that Mrs. Cooper sent the boys "to work" with brown bag lunches each day. Caroline knew their lunches would be eaten by midmorning so she told the boys she would safely keep their brown bag lunches of baloney sandwiches nice and fresh and chilled in the gift shop refrigerator. It was just a little brown dorm room refrigerator having only enough room for bottles of sodas and the few lunches.

It wasn't more than a few weeks, Klem noticed the boys playing in the rowboat that Slim had donated at the beginning of the summer. Work for the boys kind of blended with fantasy playing around the boat. It was a little hard for Caroline or Klem to see much of a difference between working and playing. That was truly fine with both Caroline and Klem; the little boy laughter was certainly pleasant. Klem waited many years for grandchildren, and Caroline even only after a month of not being in the classroom missed this same enthusiasm.

"Klem," said Caroline, peering out of the paneled glass window of the gift shop, "Just look at those two boys, what imaginations they have! A few days ago, their mom stopped by and said if she had the time, she would like to make a planter from the rowboat. She wanted some help from you Klem, to get soil to fill it before she brings the starter plants. I think it would look nice but right about now however the boys sure are enjoying the old boat just the way it is."

Link mounted the bow of the little rowboat, turned toward his massive crew of thirty-five men. Standing tall with his sword held high in the air (really his garden spade), he encouraged his sailing crew (Jake) to continue through the sea.

"Come on, Jake, I mean men, land must be soon on the horizon! I know you haven't eaten in five days, and some of you have succumbed to drinking saltwater from the side of the boat but take heart."

Link was leading his men to lands and riches previously unknown to the people of the old European civilization now hundreds of nautical miles away.

"I, I, sir. We will follow our captain to the land of milk and honey!"

Somehow it didn't matter in their minds how the 1400s European explorers and the story of the Israelites in the Bible got mixed together. It was boy playing and anything and everything happens. It just makes sense. No one was there to point out little mistakes in the details.

Chapter 15

Fun with Klem and Jane

July 5 was Klem and Jane's thirty-fifth wedding anniversary, and Klem had promised that he would take the day off and spend it with his lovely wife. Jane typically wanted Klem to make up the itinerary for their days off. It seemed that when both were younger, and when a day was made just for them, neither could stay in bed to sleep any later. They always planned to do so, but God made young bodies with more energy. Now both in their mid-sixties, nine o'clock in the morning surely felt mighty fine in bed.

A few years ago, the Watercrests splurged and bought themselves a bread maker. Jane would put the dough and ingredients together in the machine the night before. That is just what they did, and the timer turned on the machine promptly at 6:30 a.m. The smell of freshly baked bread was wafting into their bedroom, making the appetite tingle in a strange and wonderful fashion. It also gave a complete feeling of peace and contentment, a nice way to start any day.

While savoring the delicious taste of the cranberry walnut bread, Klem had visions of how they could celebrate their wedding anniversary.

"Klem, my dear, what are you thinking?"

"Oh, nothing. What are you thinking, Jane?"

"You can't answer a question with a question, Klem! I asked you first. What are you thinking?

"Oh, all right. You know except for when Glenn and I went to Manny Lighthouse a few weeks ago, you and I haven't gone there in ages. What do you think? Should we travel up that way for the day? The weather forecast here in the paper shows a sun face, only a few clouds and seventy-eight degrees. No chance of rain."

"That sounds delightful, Klem. By the way, you never elaborated on your trip with Glenn to Manny Lighthouse. Did you two boys have fun?"

"Well, yes. It was nice to be together. You know, father and son."

"Klem, that's nice, I know. But that isn't what I mean. Exactly what did you boys do?"

"Oh, this and that, you know, two guys following their noses for the day. We had ice cream at Pat's Ice Cream Parlor, umm… twice if I remember right, once before going to Manny Light and once after."

"Oh, I see. Say, Klem, dear, did you read any signs while at the lighthouse? You know any warning signs?"

Now at this point, Klem knew he was balancing between saying the truth and changing the subject. He had been married way too long to Jane to know that she must have heard something from that outing. But how? Jane had already been in bed when they arrived back home that evening.

"You know, Jane, it would be nice if you could say what you know, if that is what you are leading to with this discussion."

Klem put down his third freshly buttered slice of bread. It somehow would not taste as good until this whole thing would be resolved. Hopefully, the bread would still be somewhat warm after all of this ended.

"All right, Klem. You know I have always admired your truthfulness, one of the reasons I married you, darling."

Klem thought this just can't be good, maybe the coffee mug he had in his clutch should be set down next to his breakfast plate as well. Trying to lighten his spirit, Klem looked at the thin rose hip branches through the kitchen breakfast room window.

A carpenter bee was circulating around the red blossoms, thinking about whether to land its heavy body on one of them. Klem wished they could trade places with each other for the next fifteen minutes.

"Yes, I know you admire my macho way about me."

"Klem, don't change the subject. You know I am talking about being truthful with each other."

"Jane, dear, I am truthful with you. Maybe I just left out some details."

Now at this point, Klem was feeling he had betrayed his lovely wife since he never told her how he and Glenn jumped the sign and nearly killed themselves, climbing like superheroes around the rocks of Manny Lighthouse.

"Klem, it just so happens that the day you decided to tempt God and go climbing where you know darn well you should not have gone was the same day of Caroline's fifth-grade field trip to the lighthouse. All twenty-seven fifth graders of Caroline's class saw the whole thing. The next school day, Caroline had to deliver a special lesson to her class on obeying signs. She made everyone in her class make posters supporting this exact thing. You should have seen some of the posters. Caroline brought them over to the house after school. One of the posters shows you falling into the ocean with a manatee biting your butt! The following week, she decided to do a lesson about sea life in the south and sea life up here in the north. Imagine a manatee up here and being a carnivore at that!"

Jane pushed her chair away from the table, pulled her napkin off from her lap, and walked over to Klem who was looking less festive.

"I love you, darling, and can't imagine not living with you, at least not for a good twenty-five more years for heaven's sake!"

With this parting of the subject, she massaged his neck and shoulders; and since it was their anniversary, she bent over and nibbled at his right ear lobe with her front teeth.

"Hey, big guy, it's our anniversary. Let's have some fun!"

Klem knew he had it coming, but that he was now forgiven.

"I love you too, Jane. Let's head up north now?"

"You mean the bedroom or Manny Light?"

Chapter 16

Out and About

BELLPORT MAINE IS A WONDERFUL seaport. Its neighborhoods are in the hills where most homes have wonderful views of the bay. As one strolls down the hills to the waterfront, shops of all kinds line the cobblestone streets. Many of the businesses have one-of-a-kind flags with their logo flowing from the side of their doors. Each store, bakery, or restaurant is so inviting, and most have some nautical theme. One particular store Klem liked was a chocolate candy store. Chocolate castings of all kinds could be admired. The aroma of freshly poured dark chocolate almost made Klem float off the cobble stones and right into the shop. Both Klem and Jane's favorite chocolate had chunks of sea salt mixed within as it was made into nicely sized bars of delight. As if the dark chocolate wasn't tasty enough, when the tongue found a cube of sea salt, the chocolate flavor seemed to intensify and dance in one's mouth.

"Darling, Klem, they have our favorite again, the kind with the sea salt. And guess what?"

Jane, acting like a schoolgirl again, melting away fifty or more years from her frame, took the wrapped chocolate bar and put it up to her ear.

"Klem, you can actually hear the ocean!"

Once down at the harbor, the restaurants became more numerous. They went to a lobster restaurant where each thick wooden table had a hole in the center, about six inches across. It didn't take either of them very long to learn that just below the hole in the table was a pot sitting on the floor. This of course was the convenient place to slide their discarded lobster pieces from the table top and into the hole and the pot below.

"Klem, how nice, we can enjoy our lobster meat prizes and dunk them in the melted butter, and we don't have to look at the antenna, shell pieces, and eyes. We have to come here again. I'm having so much fun being with you today, my love. After our meal, can we walk along the waterfront?"

Klem and Jane walked to Plumb Street, the last street that emptied onto the waterfront. Most of the times, they held hands, but at this time, Jane could not control her lightheartedness and actually skipped like a school grader just ahead of her husband. Klem drank in her motions. He loved every square inch of her and loved to see each muscle move in perfect agreement. Jane had shed off the daily inhibitions not caring if people were laughing at her or with her.

"Come on, Klem! Catch up. I think I see the mail boat getting ready to cast off. Maybe we can make it on board!"

Klem broke loose from his measured gate and joined in the fun of feeling so very young again. He sucked in the afternoon air, filling his lungs with the salt air, the freshness of God's best creation. Klem loved the simple joys, even finding pleasure in the hollow sounds of the pier made by their shoes as they pranced toward the ticket booth.

Jane spoke first and for both of them. "Can we get tickets for the mail boat before it takes off? We can hurry if need be!"

The ticket person said that they had five or ten more minutes as it was to leave the pier at 2:00 p.m.

"That will be fifteen dollars each, or if you might happen to be senior citizens, twelve dollars and fifty cents each. But you will have to be over fifty-five years old," she said with her teenage voice and perfect smile.

"Oh, we have been over fifty-five for quite some time now. Klem, give the nice girl twenty-five dollars. Isn't she so sweet. She wasn't really sure if we were old enough."

The "nice girl" was Sandy, a perfect example of youthful freshness and innocence. She was well suited for her summer job of official mail boat ticket taker. Tourists were drawn to her charisma and pleasantness. From her, they would have purchased tickets to see a wet basement. Sandy enjoyed people of all ages but especially liked to see the people's dogs who were traveling along with their owners. The mail boat connected the islands to the port and made the trip several times each day. Those who made one of the towns on an island their home used the mail boats like a bus to go shopping in Bellport.

So, on these special outings, when their dogs came along, both owners and pets could enjoy the whole process. Once the boat eased away from port, even the unruliest breeds found the vibrations on the boat's deck soothing. Once inside, they would lay down, with front legs stretched out with their precious heads in between each paw. If someone walked passed, the pets would look up for a moment since frequent passengers carried small dog biscuits in their pocket for them. After a few crunches and a wave from the tip of a tail as a thank you, their heads found their paws again for the rest of the trip.

Jane and Klem stayed on the outside deck so they could see the entire waterfront move away from them as the water churned under the bow. Now, the salt air mixed with the smell of creosol preservative from the deck and pilings. In a few minutes, Klem and Jane also smelled the diesel fumes from the hardworking mail boat engines. It was amazing how the props could churn up the seawater so aggressively as the boat made its journey. After only a few minutes, they were off at sea and the seagulls would follow above the wake the entire way.

"Klem, isn't it beautiful? I hope there is an ocean in heaven. How could God make anything better?" Jane looked up into the sky and said, "God, You don't have to do anything more for heaven. This is the best."

And with that, Jane untied her hat ribbon from under her chin and allowed her silver hair to flow down to her shoulders. Like a suncatcher, each strand of her hair mesmerized Klem. He could get lost in her gleaming waves of hair.

Klem and Jane knew throughout the years of their marriage that they would mellow. The first years of breathless excitement whenever they met would lessen for sure. They didn't want that to change, but they knew it was just the way it would happen. But then there were moments like these, and all those feelings would surface again for a short but ever so wonderful visit.

Jane had both hands on the curved boat railing and was drinking in the salt air, which by this time had cooled to a pleasant chill. Klem, standing closely behind her, pulled her even closer with his arms fully around her. No words needed to be exchanged, and in fact, none were spoken. They were one with each other. No one else had ventured to stay on the outside deck. One by one, the passengers went inside to absorb the warmth, the warmth that was solely created by the humming boat engines of the hull below. So, this mail boat traveling from Big Harbor to the islands on God's beautiful blue ocean was made just for them, and they shared it together, feeling the warmth of each other's body. They cruised in silence between them, watching small islands going by, the mail boat sailing along to the next landing.

This island port called Rockland was full of long needle pines, parted by a narrow two-lane winding road. Right at the single dock nestled a general store, gas station, and across the street a country restaurant with enough room inside for six red-and-white checkered tables. As seen from the narrow street, above the bay window is a sun-faded, hand-painted sign that Klem could just make out. It proclaimed "The sea is His and He made it, and His hands formed the dry land," a quote from the good Bible. Klem and Jane remained on the boat, which stayed moored for only fifteen minutes before returning to the city. All is well with the world.

The mail boat found its way back to port, turning its props in reverse to cut speed and then mooring up to the side of the pier with a light bump. The ropes were thrown over the dock cleat, synched up carefully by the dock hands, and a small ramp was placed for debarking passengers and dogs.

"Jane, my dear, I think you should accompany your man friend with a drive along the coast."

Klem took off his yellow straw hat and with theatrical flair bowed before his woman for further enticement."

"Well, my good sir," Jane replied, "I am not sure I know you that well. Would that be appropriate for a woman of my dignified background? Just what are your intensions? Are they truly honorable?"

"I come from only the best of stock, my lady, and I assure you, my background speaks for itself. You can trust my intensions."

"Mr. Watercrest, you can hold my hand to help me into you motor vehicle if you like. Mind you, I just said for the easement of entry into your motorcar, is that what you call this?"

"Mrs. Watercrest, may I be so bold to call you Jane? It would be my privilege to do so."

"Well, I think that would be rather nice, as long as I can call you Klem, if that is not too forward, dear, I mean Mr. Watercrest?"

With those fun formalities finalized, Jane and Klem took off, hugging the nearest road to the coast as they traveled north. Every few miles or even less, the coast of Maine changes enough that they knew to pull over and take in the diverse coastline. The sight of crashing surf against the rocky cliffs never grew old in their lives. Only about thirty miles up, they found an area where the rocks were well worn from the constant sea lapping.

"Klem," Jane tugged at her husband who was at the wheel, "There is a spot where we can park. Let's go out on those smooth rocks and watch the ocean!"

"Sounds nice. I have some beach towels in the trunk."

"Oh, Klem, when you get the towels, I'll get some drier sheets from the glovebox. Could you get one towel for each of us? Trish Lowell said putting one dryer sheet in your back pocket keeps the mosquitoes and other flying insects away."

Klem replied, "Yes, we talked about bringing drier sheets before, but it was you who remembered them. At least I thought of the towels!"

"You know, Klem, between the two of us, we have one good working brain."

Once on the rocks, it was easy to find a comfortable place to share. By this time, the sun was sinking in its path across the sky, but the rocks retained the warmth of the day. After a while, sitting cross-legged led to legs outstretched and then followed by a full recline. Klem rolled one beach towel into a pillow and, lifting Jane's head, placed it underneath.

"How's that, sweetheart?"

By this time, they had stopped the Victorian play acting. Again, Klem looked at his lovely wife who had shared the last thirty-five years together. They raised two successful daughters and equally successful son together. Sometimes, they did without so that their three children could have opportunities that both Jane and Klem did not have growing up. It was all worth it. Klem felt that success was not just having financial independence, but truly following what the good Lord has taught us 2000 years ago.

Many times, Klem thought that it sure would have been nice if God gave an owner's manual to parents after they brought their newborn home from the hospital. It would have made life so much easier for baby and parents. Since that was not the case, Jane and Klem would pray at night asking God to protect their children. Their second request was for help in guiding their three children as they matured through their lives.

Jane and Klem knew that God would give them the right words to say. They only had to listen to God. Only after your life is nearly over can you look back and see how you did. It's a little hard to measure your endeavors while living within them. Finding the right man for their daughters and the right woman for their son was always a shared concern for Klem and Jane. When the time came for their children to find what they thought was their "one and only love," both Klem and Jane believed in one pretty good philosophy.

They said, "Always remember that dating is an interview process. Look for both good and the not-so-good qualities in the people you go out with."

To their two daughters, Beth and Mary, they said, "See how your boyfriend treats his mother."

To their son Glenn, they said, "See how your girlfriend treats her father."

Continuing, they said, "That is how you will be treated after you get married."

This sounds so simple, but Jane and Klem saw this to be true every time with children of dating age. It was worth repeating over several times whenever they thought it was timely.

On a different note, Jane told their three children another thing every time they left for college. Packing their car, Jane had a chance to remind each one, "You know your dad and I love you very much, and I know you heard this before from me but I mean it. No matter what you do, always represent your family well. Secondly, don't do anything you would not want to read about yourself if it was printed in the next morning's newspaper."

Klem took the blue-and-white beach towel and made a pillow for himself. Within minutes, both sixty-five-year-old lovers were part awake, part asleep, and then after a few minutes mostly more asleep.

The tide was coming in, and with each successive wave, the spray of foam and saltwater got closer and closer to the sleeping two on the rocks. It only took one good pulse for a nicely sized splash to completely bathe the rock next to them, sending ocean water ten or more feet into the air. After an instant, the spray rained down directly on Jane and Klem. After this abrupt awaking, both sat up, looked at each other all dripping wet, laughed out loud, and scurried off their perch and headed to their waiting car.

"Klem, let's turn the heat on. Yuck, damp clothes. We should have known better."

To this, Klem replied in his mind, "When did I hear that before?"

Driving along during this time of twilight, the setting sun became "eaten" by the coastal cliffs. A brief time later, when driving through a clearing among the hills, they were able to enjoy the red sky and the sun one more time again. On this little getaway excursion, however, this scene was repeated again and again for Klem and Jane.

"Oh, Klem look. There's a crescent-shaped beach down there on my side. Let's stop to see the best of the setting sun."

As they drove closer, they saw a parking lot with at least five dozen cars. People had made their way onto the sand and walked onto the flat damp, hard-packed beach. From here, forty or more people, all who seemed to Jane and Klem to be over sixty years old, gathered here. This was their normal ritual in this area. The sun's golden rays turned to pink and then a deep red, now reflecting into the clouds that sent the colors overhead for miles. The whole crowd stood with total respect, remaining silent taking in God's final triumph for this day that He made.

Then, as soon as the very last sliver of orange sunk below the horizon, without any signal, the whole group of admirers let out a huge cheer, clapping their hands, while others were waving their hats or scarves. Instinctively, Jane and Klem joined in with the cheers. Then, as soon as it happened, one by one, everyone turned from the ocean and retraced their steps found in the sand. Even after so many years of Maine living, neither Jane nor Klem knew about this ritual at this littlest beach, nestled between the rocky cliffs. Klem thought to himself, "These are my people!"

Just before Klem placed the car into reverse, his hand on the floor shifter, Jane placed her hand on top of Klem's, looked into his eyes, and simply said, "Thank you."

Chapter 17

Back Home

If any new stock items for the lighthouse gift shop arrived, it was by FedEx, and it always came on a Monday. Today was Monday, and Klem and Caroline were expecting a larger-than-normal delivery. The big white truck slowly came to view as it took the upward grade to the lighthouse.

"I'll get it this time, Caroline," said Klem as he put down his cleaning cloth that he used for the windows of the gift shop.

"I think this is a large delivery this time around. I'm going to get the two-wheeled dolly from the back to haul it in here."

The fact is that this was a large order, including DVDs of U.S. lighthouses, tabletop miniature lighthouses, jewelry, buoy chimes, greeting cards, books, posters, and various candies. The most cherished stock were various pieces of hand-scratched scrimshaw. Originally, many years ago, sailors, passing the time while onboard, would scratch nautical scenes such as mermaids, sailing vessels, and lighthouses into white whale bones. They would then rub the piece with ink and wipe off the excess, and the scene almost became three-dimensional. Some of these were no less than masterpieces to be sure.

Klem walked out, hopped onto the truck's running board, and leaned a little into the opened driver's side window.

"Hi, Pete. How's it going since I saw you last?"

"Not bad, Klem. How about you?"

Klem hopped back down on the ground, took each of the boxes from Pete, stacked them on the dolly, and then signed the receipt.

"See you the next time around, Pete!"

With that, Klem pulled the dolly with its treasures along the brick walkway and propped it next to the first of three concrete steps. Caroline opened the screen door to receive the first box. Once the boxes were inside, Caroline motioned to Klem to sit down next to her by the cash register.

"Say, Klem, I wanted to talk about something with you."

Caroline's usually bright tone was just under her usual cheerful way of talking.

"Klem, last month, when I took my class to the Manny Lighthouse on a field trip, we saw two men climbing where they should not have been. After looking through my binoculars, I saw that they were you and Glenn. The next day, I told Jane about it, and this has made me very guilty since I did not just go and talk with you first. I don't know how many times I have wanted to confess that I went to Jane about this and not you. I am so sorry Klem."

"Goodness gracious, hang me out to dry. I don't want to revisit this whole thing again. Caroline, don't worry. It's fine. It all worked out and is all history now. I am sorry that you have been carrying around any guilt about this for a month."

"Thanks, Klem. I'm glad you are not mad at me or anything. I do have to say that I was able to make some great lessons for my class from the experience."

Klem just answered in a quiet tone, "Yes, I know." He wasn't much for facial expressions, but with Caroline's response, he rolled his blue eyes above his wire-rim glasses.

"I heard about the posters they created. Well, let's get to these packages. They won't unwrap themselves and jump on the shelves without some help from us."

Changing the subject, Caroline said, "Speaking of help, here come the Cooper boys now. I see they have their lunches with them. Why do boys have to do pointless things like swing their lunch bags over their heads and other silly gyrations? Look! They are pushing each other, almost off the path as they are walking."

"Caroline, you should be used to this with teaching fifth grade."

"Use to it, but not understanding it."

Klem, eyeing them from his vantage point and peering through the gift shop screen door, greeted Link and Jake with a friendly "Hello!"

With their typical response, both boys answered with energetic voices and in complete unison, "Hi, Mr. Watercrest!"

Then, Link continued, "We're going to play on the boat again. Is that all right?"

Caroline turned to Klem as she opened another package with her box cutter, "Not going to make much money if all they do is play."

With a little smile, Klem replied, "Didn't I say that was going to be short-lived? Hey, they are twelve years old, and it is their summer vacation. In fact, I have asked their mother, Pat, if she would use her talents and make a flower bed out of the boat. She thought that would be lovely, and she is already arranging it in her head. So, the boys will soon have to find another way to have fun. Maybe by that time, Jake's new front bicycle wheel will be in, and they will once again take to the wind with their bikes."

Back outside by the boat, Link took the lead with their story line pulling himself up onto the front rim of the boat. Jake sat on the wooden bench in the rear of the rowboat. With hands grasping the bench on either side, he managed to get the little boat rocking left and right. After rocking on the ground for a few minutes, puffs of dirt were sent a little airborne. This delighted Link immensely.

Pointing to the puffs of dirt, Jake announced in a loud captain's voice, "There she blows! A whale of immense size and strength! Hold your own, men. We can get her this time. Mind you men, heed my warnings. Look out for the tail of the whale! One hit from her giant tail, and this ship is a goner and we will all be fish food! Men! Row with all your might all the way to parting of the Red Sea up yonder."

JAY DIEDRECK

And with that, two little boys's imagination took over, and the great whale hunt was born.

After the task of restocking the shelves, items that did not have room were then placed in the basement of the gift shop. Klem thought that he would take the remaining boxes down and then have his lunch. He had to go out the front door around the side, past the Cooper brothers and "their boat," and enter the basement through metal hurricane-style doors. Klem could have used the other basement door, but this way, he had space to manage the boxes in his grasp.

The steps going down into the basement were concrete and well-worn over the years. A seventy-five-watt light bulb hung from its wire in the center of the single-room basement. Klem reached up to the bulb where there was a black Bakelite switch and twisted it to turn on the light. Over in the corner were odds and ends, leftover from day gone years. Some of the items were old life jackets, lanterns, empty red gas cans, and wooden oars. Even though the steps were concrete, the floor of the basement was only hard-packed dirt. The basement air carried a little musty odor, but not objectionable.

"Well, that's the last box of goodies. Now for some lunch," Klem said to himself.

The task winded him a little more than he expected and surprised him a little.

"Oh, to be young again like the Cooper boys, but with the wisdom of sixty-five years of living. Now that would be an improvement on this old soul of mine."

Klem paused at the top of the cellar stairs looking at the Cooper boys's playing activity. A few miles beyond, Klem saw the dinghies that the sailing club rookies used for practicing turning maneuvers. Once mastering the small sailboats, the same techniques came into play with full-size sailboats. Races were held in August where the coveted sailing trophy would earn many a bragging right.

When 4:30 p.m. arrived, Klem had to come to a painful realization. He knew the lighthouse had to be repaired on the outside and then repainted. Some of the stucco was missing, and the exposed stones had to be pointed. In some sections, parts of the old lime-stone mortar mix had to be removed and replaced with fresh mortar. This was something Klem could not do. Maybe twenty years ago, he would have rented some scaffolding and wooden planks to build up vertically along the outside of the lighthouse, but now this was out of the question.

By this hour, the Cooper boys had decided that it was getting close to dinner time and had headed down the hill to their house to see what their mom was cooking in the kitchen. A few minutes later, Klem and Caroline locked up the gift shop and lighthouse and together walked to the parking lot. Caroline always drove since she lived several miles away. Klem said goodbye and started his short walk to his home in town. He knew Jane would be waiting for his return and would ask him how his day was. Looking back on his day, Klem thought it was pleasant, but he had a lump in his throat think-ing of his limitations. He floundered a little thinking if he should tell Jane about his concern.

"Hi, Klem. How was your day, dear?"

Jane heard the familiar sound of the screen door lightly taping closed behind Klem as he walked through the house into the back kitchen. She was still uplifted from their outing of the previous day.

Klem answered, "It went well, honey. Thanks for asking."

"But I always ask. You know that. You are my hunk of a man, and I want to know. You remember I want to be connected at the hip with you."

Jane's words were a little less comforting, and he certainly didn't feel like a "hunk of a man" right now.

"I think I will just sit here while you finish what you're doing, unless you want some help."

Klem tried to make the tone in his voice mirror Jane's, but it fell short.

"Klem, what's the matter?"

Sitting down her wooden spoon on the edge of her Tupperware mixing bowl, she dusted off her hands on the front of her flower print apron and pulled a kitchen chair next to him. She was now sitting and facing her husband. Something was truly wrong.

Jane knew that Klem needed some time to muster up the energy to express his thoughts. She looked into his steel blue eyes searching for why he was so somber. She remained silent and patient, but she knew he would come around in a few minutes.

"Jane, I truly don't think I can keep the lighthouse going much longer."

Jane did not want to put words in his mouth, so she remained the tender recipient of his thoughts.

"I can tend to the light refueling, the lighthouse grounds, and of course the gift shop and other things like washing windows and giving tours. But the exterior is quite beyond my abilities."

"Well, I should say so. Klem, you have mentioned a few times about having to do some outside repairing. Be honest with me Klem, you know I haven't encouraged you to that kind of extensive repair work. Hey, babe, you're not thirty years old anymore."

"But I can't just let it go to disrepair, honey! You see, it's quite a dilemma and I am pretty upset about it, maybe more that you know."

Jane looked at her man. She knew he was proud, but time had placed limitations on all of us, and Klem was presently feeling a lot of it.

Chapter 18

Help at the Light

"Klem, I love you to pieces, and let's think about this tonight. Let me finish the tuna casserole and put it in the oven to brown. We are a team darling, and we can figure this out."

Klem had a little tear in the corner of his eye, which he hoped would not show his weakness to his wife. Maybe after the tuna casserole and a little glass of Chardonnay, he would feel more stark-worthy. Jane's casserole always had a nice crunchy crust; tonight, she placed a little more grated sharp cheese on top. She would remember to check on it through the oven window several times during its last few minutes under the broiler and pull it just as it started to bubble.

Dinner had an effect of empowering both of them, so after the dishes were washed and placed on the sink dish rack, Jane and Klem went into the living room to continue with the earlier conversation.

Klem still didn't feel they could resolve anything, but unknown to Klem, Jane had been brainstorming silently throughout dinner.

Jane knew that any idea of hers had to make Klem feel that he was part of the plan or he might resist. He was awfully stubborn in his own way, but so was she. Jane came from a part Irish and English background and could stand her ground when she needed to. Her lovely maiden name was changed by the immigration officers of Ellis Island when, several generations ago, her ancestors were being processed. Immigration officers meant well, but could not take the time to spell all these strange European names correctly. The masses of immigrates constantly pressed in toward the processing desks as soon as the boat unloaded its human cargo.

Jane knew this story well. As a young girl, she decided if she was there, facing those immigration officers of Ellis Island, she would had insisted on the correct spelling. From the first time she heard the story, she developed her stubborn nature, maybe just to make up for this injustice of her name change.

"Klem, I've been mulling over about what you said, and I would like to see if you might think this may be a good idea, or not."

Klem fidgeted in his overstuffed chair and pushed his hands along the arm rests as if to smooth out the wrinkles in the worn leather.

"Now, Klem, honey, promise not to say 'no' right off the bat, but just think about it a little first. Okay?"

After the appropriate amount of silence, Klem responded accordingly, feeling like a naughty six grader in Caroline's class waiting for scolding in front of his classmates.

Repeating his wife's request, Klem replied "okay" with very little enthusiasm.

Several years ago, Jane had single-handedly came to the rescue of the lighthouse. Quite unexpectedly, the Watercrests had received a letter from the federal government. It was very impressive, having the seal of the White House and all. The lighthouse grant from the federal government was going to cease. It had been renewed several times by Sarah, but that year, the funding had dried up.

Before the need to apply for financial grants the U.S. Coast Guard owned and operated the light, in fact from the day it was built. It was now up to Port James residents to find some way to financially support their light if they wanted to keep it functioning.

The federal government would fence it off from the public. People would only be able to see it from a distance, and eventually, the old light would have to be demolished for safety reasons. A historical plaque sponsored by the coast guard would be erected where once a proud 160-foot beacon once stood.

Jane paid a visit to the Tucker's home to speak with Sarah. With the U.S. government letter in her handbag, she lifted the knocker on the front door and then peered in to see if she was home. It wasn't too long before Sarah's form took shape, making Jane to step away from the door so as not to appear that she was looking in her home.

"Well, hello, Jane. Come right on in. Please don't mind my appearance. I was finally getting around to cleaning up the old pile of cinders from last winter's fires in the fireplace."

Jane's mind flashed for a moment thinking of how the lighthouse might become a pile of rubble if their town was not successful in saving the light.

"Sarah, I just got this official letter today. It pretty much explains everything. We need to do something."

So, with that, Jane's presentation at the next town meeting was placed on the agenda, and the group calling themselves "Friends of Port James Lighthouse" was born. A budget of a few thousand dollars for yearly maintenance would be needed, since the lighthouse would be open to the public from Memorial Day at the end of May to Labor Day, the first week of September. Then, another certain amount would have to be decided and voted on for staffing to keep the lantern lit, grounds keeping, and insurance. A certain amount of money would be raised each year from entrance fees collected from those who wanted to climb up to the top.

Jane actually spearheaded this whole endeavor. She first enlisted mildly interested townspeople with a promise of peach pie with rose hip drizzle, if they stayed to the end of the entire meeting. Her pie had previously won her a gold ribbon at the county fair, not the trophy mind you since the trophy went to Zoe Chase.

Zoe might have just bribed the four male judges at the fair. She made it known to each of them that if her strawberry short-cake just happened to take the trophy, then each of the men would be welcomed to use her vintage Jaguar sports car for an entire day. This arrangement would occur on any summer day as long as they brought the vintage auto back, washed, and waxed. This way Zoe was assured the Bake-Off trophy, and in the process, she obtained four free washes and waxes for her little English four-wheeled baby. Zoe named her sports car Charles, after of course Prince Charles of Wales.

The new recruits of the "Friends of Port James Lighthouse" at first were less enthusiastic about their future mission as they were for the enjoyment at the end of the meeting. Jane's warm peach pie with toasted brown sugar crust and sweet rose hip drizzle lightly poured over the checkerboard crust top did wonders for their membership.

Jane knew it was worth picking the bowls and bowls of ripe rose hips to sustain membership numbers. The peach pie was truly a labor of love. Making the drizzle, Jane downed yellow Playtex gloves to protect her fingers from the thorny stems that guarded the rose hip fruit. After cutting the rose hips into quarters, she would boil the concoction for over an hour. Then, she added a pinch of pectin to lightly thicken her reward, adding corn syrup for sweetness. This made the whole sweet divine mixture a beautiful clear red. As word got out that Jane's dessert was part of the agenda, her small group of three expanded to twelve, quite respectable for a small seaside village.

All this occurred fifteen years ago, and now Klem's loving wife was once again at his side, "connected at the hip" thinking of a way to help her aging husband.

"You know, Klem, I was reading in the Maine magazine that came last month that Youngtown's Marine College has several internships for their curriculum. I read that in their junior year, every student had to work one of these internships before advancing to their senior year.

One internship requires students to work on the 1850 historical merchant sailship currently dry-docked at the marina where the mail boat slip was located. Remember seeing that last week darling? Another is working at one of Maine's lighthouses doing all sorts of tasks from general housekeeping to more extensive repair work. So what do you think? It's up to you of course, but maybe we could find out if our little structure could be one for the college student's internship."

Jane could see that Klem had formed a little frown in response to her idea. She knew that it was time to back off and let Klem sleep on it.

"Darling, why don't you promise me to just think about it a little? Right for now, let's have some peach pie for dessert and then call it a night."

Klem had waved his stubbornness off a little since he knew his limitations. Actually, he was thinking about the feasibility of Jane's idea even as soon as it took him to rise from his favorite chair by the fireplace and go back into the kitchen for Jane's dessert. Of course, he couldn't let Jane know he was truly thinking more positively about her idea. It would have to wait for tomorrow's new light of day to tell her what he thought.

Somehow, evening concerns are sometimes magnified in one's mind, and the expression of "sleeping on it" is more than that. Sleep, however, has a way of clearing things up, and an answer to a difficult question in the morning becomes a rather easy "yes or no." The very next morning, Klem woke up with a "yes" on his lips. With a feeling of triumph and great insight, he announced to his lovely wife that they should at least look into having some help from the college students.

"Very well, my dear. That sounds like a great idea." Jane was already in the kitchen, while Klem was finishing up in the bathroom. They were talking from one room to the other. Shaking out the bread from the bread maker machine and making coffee using a Nantucket-flavored K-cup, she couldn't resist rolling her eyes along with a smile. Sometimes Klem was easy to guide, but she didn't take him for granted.

"Breakfast is almost ready, my dear. Are you done shaving?"

Klem had tried using an electric shaver several times in his life, but only after a test run of a week or so, he would always go back to the shaving cream and blade. He washed his face, letting the excess shaving cream go down the sink along with the whiskers. Patting his face dry, he came out bare-chested into the kitchen.

A little startled, Jane stopped her breakfast preparation for a moment and said, "Good heavens, Klem! It's not like I don't like the view. I just can't imagine what the neighbors would think if they saw you."

"Well, they shouldn't be looking into our windows, my lady. Besides, it's nothing more than they would see at the beach."

"Jane, I think I will wear my fishing shirt today. Is it out of the wash?"

Jane wondered how much she would get paid if she charged for all the work she did around the homestead. She liked Klem's collection of fishing shirts because they could be a little wrinkled and still look fine.

"Klem, if you don't find one of those shirts hanging in your closet, look on the clothesline in the backyard. But for heaven's sake, don't linger. Just quickly put it on. You know, the neighbors would probably say, 'There goes poor Klem wandering around without a shirt again, looking lost,' or something worse."

"You're funny, sweetheart. What's for breakfast?"

It was several weeks after Jane contacted the provost of Youngtown's Marine College when she and Klem received a thick manila envelope in the mail. They both opened it up at the breakfast table and started sorting out the application.

After about a half hour, with a little glazed look, Klem finally said to his wife, "Goodness gracious, great balls of tar! Look at all the paper work just for some lousily help. Can't they just say it sounds like a great idea and send some of their students our way?"

"Now, Klem, you know that there are additional insurance issues, college curriculum requirements, a total estimation for hours to complete the job, OSHA regulations, and probably many other things. There will have to be a representative from the college who will come out to interview you and look at the work that has to be done. So be patient, dear. We can get through all of this."

A little worried, Klem responded back, "But what if I don't answer the questions right, or if they don't like the condition of the lighthouse? What then?"

"Klem, think of it this way, what would be the worst that could happen? The college would reject your request, and we would be back at square one. It's no worse than where we are now, and that's not so horrible."

Klem thought that was pretty good reasoning, so they set to work filling in the blanks first in pencil and then again in pen. It took several days to finish the application. Klem asked and received help from Pastor Dell. The good preacher had a flare for sermons, so the essay part about the history of the light came easy for him.

Now that it was summer, the normal craziness and demands on the Youngstown's Marine College staff were diminished quite a bit. The turnaround for the application was only a matter of a few weeks. Joyce Westman was the Curriculum Development Specialist for some of the Marine Studies, which sometimes involved restorations, beach cleanup, and wildlife preservation. She was somewhat familiar with Port James. As a child, her family vacationed here several times during the summer. Her family would always go to the lighthouse and enjoyed seeing the scenery from the top. She wondered if Klem was the same gentleman that worked the lighthouse from her childhood visits.

Pulling up to Klem and Janes's house, Joyce parked her car in the drive and unbuckled her seat belt. Taking a moment or two, she took in the older yet pristine condition of their home. Walking up the brick sidewalk, she paused to admire the flowers on either side. Straightening her blouse and skirt, she knocked on the green screen door with two raps. Looking through the screen, she saw some movement toward the front. Presuming it to be Klem, she greeted him first, opening the door with one hand and extending the other to shake his hand.

"Klem Watercrest? Your front yard is just divine! I am Joyce Westman from Youngstown's Marine College. So good to finally meet you. I truly need to talk with your wife about her flower gardens. I would like to start one myself whenever I get the time, probably next spring."

Klem was a little uncertain about all this renovation for his lighthouse and felt quite nervous as well. After all, Gray Cliff Light almost seemed to be "his" since he took care of her needs for so many years.

"Please, come in Mrs. Westman. Welcome to my home."

"Oh, please, call me Joyce. I am not in my campus office, and you are not one of the freshmen."

Her mannerism was pleasant and supportive. Klem was rather captivated by what appeared to be her genuine interest in the lighthouse.

Joyce found it a very nice diversion to get into the field, away from the daily entourage of endless paper work. In fact, it was truly like a field trip for her. She would definitely get this together for the fall term curriculum, Klem would get his help, and the college would have another internship to list in the college pamphlet for Marine Studies. Joyce was rather proud of herself in that she was able to insert a handsome colored picture of the lighthouse and the gift shop in the college curriculum catalogue.

Chapter 19

On the Way There

As THE SUMMER DAYS BLOSSOMED one after another, it seemed like no time at all that the middle of August had arrived. The Maine evenings were the warmest they would become; the temperatures would be a pleasant sixty-five degrees with a slight breeze coming off the ocean. It was always Jane who would take an assessment of how much time the two of them had spent together.

"Klem, I need another outing, just the two of us like the day trip when we went to Manny Light. We are not getting any younger, and it seems like we are always doing things for everyone else. We need, or at least I need, time with just each other."

Klem felt the same way. Somehow, he needed a little kick, but once they were pulling out of the driveway, he would start to feel a little younger again. It certainly was a gift to be able to get around and be with the one he loved. They thought a lot about Trish and her husband, Hank. Jane and he had been praying for both at night and in church with the whole congregation. He wondered how many days she had left. Such a shame. A situation like that was a kick in the pants to make sure the important things in life like relationships should be enjoyed. So that is just what they would do.

"Klem, I would love to go all the way up to Big Harbor. I have been looking on the computer, and it just looks delightful. Do you think we could take a few days off from our normal activities and 'just do it'?"

Klem thought a minute and asked Jane, "Can you check out some bed and breakfast places in Big Harbor? If there are any vacancies next week, I will arrange for one of the guys from church to keep the light going at the lighthouse for a few days while we are gone."

"Oh, Klem, do you really mean it? I'll check it out right now, darling! I can't wait!"

Nothing felt better to Klem than to have his wife excited about something they were planning to do. It truly melted away the years and made those years of working worthwhile. Not that their lives were not a blessing each and every day, but an occasional trip away from daily routines was certainly invigorating, and it helped to rediscover each other.

Jane went in the extra bedroom that doubled as a guest room to look on the Internet for house rental. Just like magic, after an hour on the computer, she found a white Victorian Bed and Breakfast home to spend four days away with her best friend. Next Tuesday, they would set to the north and explore their state a little more.

Big Harbor was 150 miles north, and usually, Klem and Jane would take the coastal route through the many small coastal towns that dotted the shore. This time, however, Jane was too excited to take four or more hours to get there, so they took U.S. Route 5.

The entrance to U.S. Route 5 was just three miles north of Port James. There were a few cars backed up waiting to feed onto the expressway, but from that point on, it would be sixty-five miles per hour. One by one, each car in front of them waited their turn and then accelerated to match the expressway speed. After a minute or more, the two sixty-five-year-old lovebirds were next in line. Klem saw a bright yellow car in front, pushed forward, and then increased his speed likewise. Within a blink of an eye, the yellow car screech to a dead stop. Klem had to brake with full force to avoid a fender bender with this car in the lead.

"Why? What in tarnation is that driver thinking?"

Klem hit his fist on the steering wheel, while his temper grew. Then, within a second or so, the car zoomed off onto U.S. Route 5.

Jane and Klem have ridden with many friends, and an occurrence like this would bring unflattering names to the "stupid" driver.

Somehow, there is a primeval need in all of us to clear our nerves by calling names. It usually feels better afterward, but sometimes it just lengthens the negative feelings that have resulted. A few years ago, Jane decided to call drivers like this "stupid" one different assortment of names. Instead of nasty names, Jane decided to use dessert names. Right now, this was the perfect situation for the dessert calling. Klem did the name calling first.

"Why that vanilla chocolate chip cookie."

Jane replied, adding a little fancier dessert, "That mocha caramel drizzle frappe!"

"That strawberry upside down strudel!" Klem continued.

"What a chocolate swirl pineapple fruit cup!"

By this time, the silliness of the dessert name calling led to healing laughter between them. So with fun in their hearts, they continued on just fine.

Jane thought for a moment and said, "I hope we don't meet those two guys from the yellow car at the next rest area. I might look at them and long for something sweet on top of some nice peach ice cream."

Klem chuckled both at her thought and at the gift God had given them to deal with trivial things like that.

U.S. Route 5 is pleasant enough, and the tall pine trees on either side of the expressway are truly amazing; however, as hours go by, conversations helped to pass the time.

Jane said, "Klem can you tell me some of those funny 'one liners' that you tell our grandchildren when they are riding with us in their rather uncomfortable car seats?"

"Are you sure you want to hear them? After all, they are for the kids."

"Oh, Klem, entertain me, you big hunk. I find them pretty funny too!"

Klem found it hard to think of even one of the funny things that he had entertained the grandchildren. However, after a while, one funny liner would lead to triggering his memory and another followed. Soon, they were almost piling up inside his brain waiting impatiently to come out.

"Well, give me a minute. Let me see if I can remember one. Oh, yes, remember this? Don't tailgate a rhinoceros. They can stop faster than you ever expect."

"How about this one? Stuffed peppers shouldn't eat so much."

"Or, when I was a child, I liked to play the game pin the tail on the donkey until the donkey turned around and bit me."

"How about this one? Have twice as much time in your life. Wear two watches."

"Or when drinking, keep your nose out of your glass to avoid drowning."

Klem was on a roll, and Jane was giggling, so he continued without any more encouragement, "Before letting a polar bear in your kitchen, get his name and phone number, just in case he breaks your toaster."

"When it rains, if driver's seats faced sideways, we wouldn't need windshield wipers."

"And then there was, in the morning, avoid putting traffic jam on your toast."

"Or how about, if a bear attacks you, hand him a smartphone. He just won't know what to do with it."

"When painting a large house, instead of a ladder, use a trampoline. Or my favorite. Don't forget to wear your clothes when you are the guest speaker at a biting mosquito convention."

"Oh, Klem Watercrest, you didn't say that to our little grandchildren!"

"Jane, it's not anything worse than what they hear on the school bus. Hey, I just thought of another one. While at work, have fun and sit on a copier and fax yourself to Florida for the day!"

"Klem, that's to stay in this car and go no further!"

"If a coworker doesn't like you, feed them to a walrus."

"Stop, Klem, that's just plain awful! Do you have any more?"

"Have fun at lunch. Drink the milk from the bottom of your glass first."

"If you have a headache, give it to someone else."

"If cattails grow outside, where does the rest of the cat grow?"

"If the shoulder of the road is on the side, where is its bottom?"

"Klem, stop your terrible! Any more?"

"Always look for the good in everyone else or just throw chicken soup at them."

"If you bump your knee on a crowded bus, avoid rubbing it. It may be someone else's."

"Have fun one morning when getting out of bed. Jump directly into a pot of orange Jell-O."

"Klem, you better stop or we will miss our exit. But thanks for the lift. Remember though not all of them are for our grandchildren to hear. Okay?

"Yes, dear. You know I am very careful what I say around them. I will be sure not to tell them that all day long, park benches meet a lot of asses."

"Klem, you just missed our exit!"

Chapter 20

Big Harbor

BIG HARBOR IS JUST A perfect seaside harbor town. The main street is located on a gentle hill that leads to the waterfront deep enough for ocean liners to dock. There is a grassy park along the ocean walkway leading up to a grand white gazebo. Wonderful shops are nestled on either side of the main street. One of these shops sells real beautiful scrimshaw. Unique restaurants with either ocean or street views are dotted throughout, facing the gas lamp sidewalks of yesteryears.

"Oh, Klem, there is so much to see. But let's find our bed and breakfast first. I can't wait to see what it looks like, as well as our room."

Big Harbor has several bed and breakfasts, mostly in the Victorian-style architecture. Each home boasts of their own gazebo decorated with fancy gingerbread molding, cupolas with little lights inside, and generous wraparound porches with white wicker rocking chairs to enjoy the sea breezes.

For four wonderful nights, their bed and breakfast was one of these grand old Victorian ladies. Her curved windows matched the round turrets of the front living room and dining room. The entire home was set among flowering gardens with little reflection pools, each containing several goldfish. A serpentine brick walkway greeted the guests leading from the sidewalk to the front steps.

Klem and Jane again held each other's hands as they walked up the front stairs onto the porch and then into the grand foyer. All the floors were made of wide plank oak with a chestnut border, secured with contrasting dark wood doweling.

Although there were plenty of stained-glass windows throughout, most were clear glass allowing sunny streams of light to visit each room. The living room fireplace was the centerpiece of the room. It was made of cherrywood having carved ocean waves etched in the rich wood just below the mantle. Fluted columns on either side with Corinthian column heads helped to hold up the marble mantle, keeping everything in nice proportion. An antique Seth Thomas clock, which needs hand-winding every six days, was displayed on the center of the mantle. Every morning, fresh flowers arranged in ceramic vases were newly placed before the first guest came down for breakfast.

Jane spoke first, "I can't believe this will be our place for the next four days! What do we do first? Should we find someone?"

It wasn't a moment later and the proprietor came from a side room and greeted them with an extended hand and laughing smile.

"Hello, my name is Lynn. My husband Norris is currently in the back garden making a fresh flower arrangement for the breakfast room. Welcome to my home. You are our special guests. Let me see, you must be Klem and Jane Watercrest from south of Mansfield. How was your road trip? My husband and I hope you will find our seaside town pleasant. There is so much to do!"

Jane replied, "Oh yes, yes. I already want to move here!"

"Let me show you the room I selected for your stay. It is called the Puffin Room named after the cliff birds from around here. Maybe you will see some if you go along the shore. If not, you will surely see carvings of them in the gift shops on the main street."

Lynn led the way up the gracious staircase. The spindles holding the banister and railing must have been hand-lathed by meticulous wood craftsmen of yesteryears.

"The original owner of this mansion was Jason Krensoll who made his fortune in logging. He and his wife Maryann lived here for fifty-one years, raising their five children from 1810 to 1861.

They supplied most of their food from a small farm, which, now long gone, was in the back of the house. I believe it was ten acres in total. They had a few farm animals as well, not too many just enough for sustenance. You know what I mean."

Their room overlooked the side yard and was part of the round turret to the right of the home. Each room had their own bath including a small shower. Klem estimated the bath was added ten or so years ago. He based his guess on the sink fixtures he glanced from the corner of his eye.

The turret area of the room had a white wicker table and two wicker chairs with blue-and-white striped cushions. A small fresh flower bouquet was centered on the table. Its fragrance was triggered by the sunshine flowing in from the rounded windows. To the right as one entered was a four-poster king-sized bed with down feather pillows as accents on the white linen comforter. The entire bed was on a raised section of the floor so you would take the one step to get to either side of the bed.

Lynn pointed out that on the far side of the bed sat a short handmade wooden bench if Klem or Jane needed a little help to mount the bed.

"We have been told that most of our guests use the bench. When we make up the bed, we tuck the sheets in tight so our visitors don't fall. So far, we haven't lost any guests, ha! ha! If they did fall out of bed, they never 'fess up to it!' Well, I hope you enjoy your stay! Tomorrow, I will look forward for you both to meet me and my husband, Norris, for breakfast any time between 7:30 a.m. and 9:00 a.m.

Oh yes, there are some wine glasses and a selection of wine to sample in the pantry if you would like. There are also some games in the captain's chest next to the wine rack, you know like scrabble, chess, or checkers. Here are your room keys. We will look forward to hearing about your discoveries as you enjoy your days in our splendid town!

Oh yes, I almost forgot. On top of the foyer table just inside the front door are visitor maps, sample menus of area restaurants, and other things to see and do. We have a ten percent discount voucher for Grandpa George's restaurant. If you go there, be sure to take one. Tonight is an evening cruise, rain or shine, leaving our port at eight o'clock. They do a nice job. One of the sailing staff gives some of the history of the town while onboard. Well, enjoy!"

After unpacking their suitcases and hanging their several changes of clothes in the antique armoire, Jane led the way out to the hallway and waited for Klem to check his hair one more time in the mirror. "Come on, big boy. There is a whole town waiting for us. Let's go!"

By the time the two explored some of the neighborhood homes, it was time for some dinner, being 7:30 p.m.

"What do you feel like eating, Jane?" asked Klem.

"Oh, I don't know. Maybe some seafood, fresh of course, and hopefully not deep-fried."

Jane spied a cute restaurant just ahead and, skipping up to the front, looked at the menu placed in the window near the double door.

"Klem, this looks like a friendly place, and the windows are very clean."

Jane had her own theory that if a restaurant could not take the time to keep their windows clean, then their kitchen is probably in much worse shape. After all, the kitchen is not in the public eye, and so it could be quite a mess back there and not be seen.

Klem took this opportunity to lag a little behind Jane as she went up the three stone steps to read the menu. He looked with admiration of God's creation. He loved her shapely legs, fuller than those models in those current magazines at the checkout lines in the grocery stores. Her legs, back, and shoulders had a scattering of freckles throughout her golden skin. Jane had stopped trying to tan her skin by lying in the sun many years ago, but just walking into town or gardening still gave the skin color that enlisted Klem's interest. Her freckles also seemed to be more apparent when sun-kissed. Jane would always tell their grandchildren who all sported freckles that only special people have freckles.

With a quick twist, Jane looked behind her to see if Klem was looking at her. It was a quick, innocent look, and to her delight, Jane had her husband's fullest attention the whole time.

Klem finally answered Jane about the seafood restaurant. "Sounds great, sweetheart. Is it crowded?"

The first thing they encountered when walking inside was the menu also written on a chalkboard behind and above the counter. Klem and Jane gave the lady at the cash register their selection where she copied it onto a small pad of paper. When finished with their order, she reached up in front of her and secured it onto a large clip that was waiting on a wire. With one quick movement, she swung her arm sending the order and metal clip on the wire straight into the kitchen. With a bang, it hit squarely on a cowbell at the end of the wire, just above the chief who was at the stove.

Bang! Bang! For some reason, when each order was sent down the wire line eventually hitting the bell, the whole restaurant would cheer at the ring. It was a down to earth and fun place that Jane found for them to eat.

Dinner was great, as Jane ordered lazy lobster. Lazy lobster is fresh lobster meat that has been all shelled, and the only thing left was to spear the tasty pieces with a fork and dunk them in drawn butter. She mixed the morsels with her baked potato and fresh steamed broccoli. Klem had grilled Atlantic salmon with a light citrus glaze, homemade smashed potatoes, and buttered baby corn.

After paying the bill, Klem opened the door for his date. Jane was right—they needed this runaway time together.

Klem felt his wife brush next to him, pausing a moment in the doorway to the street. It truly felt good to be with her.

In that moment, Jane felt the same closeness as Klem. She whispered to herself, "Thank you, God."

After perusing several unique gift shops, they both spied a scrimshaw shop, which was next in line. The gift shop that Klem and Caroline ran back home at Gray Cliff Lighthouse had a very small selection of these carved items, mostly inexpensive. The most was twenty-five dollars.

So as not to miss any store, Jane and Klem went in. The shop was not overwhelmed with merchandise but had the largest amount of scrimshaw pocketknives, letter openers, paper weights, and other knickknacks that Klem had ever seen. Klem didn't know what to look at first. He felt like a small child with a dollar in a penny candy store.

"Klem, look at this display cabinet. These are simply beautiful!"

Most of the items she was admiring were pocketknives. Klem went over to where her body was pressing over the glass top cabinet. Just for the briefest moment, Klem caught a sense of Jane's hair. It was fresh and sweet, perfumed only by the breeze of the sea air.

"Klem, do you see anything you like here?"

Klem was rather conservative when it came to purchasing anything for himself. He had the same straw hat that he inherited from his dad many years ago. It looked cute on him, wearing it a little slanted on his brow. It was functional for him, keeping his aging eyes out of the direct sun. Jane simply liked the look.

"Well, do you see anything?"

Klem liked everything he saw, items picturing nautical waterscapes, lighthouses, mermaids, sailing vessels, and sunsets. By this time, the English-looking proprietor came over to them with a smile on his face.

"Can I take any of these out for you to see?"

"Go ahead, Klem. Look at something. I want to buy you something."

Sometimes, it is just right to let another person treat you to something special. This is one unique way that allows someone to give fulfilling joy to another. Klem looked at Jane's dancing eyes. She wanted to enjoy the gift of giving and was so happy to know Klem would cherish her gift.

"Well, this single-blade pocketknife with the sailing vessel under full mast takes my eye."

The English proprietor explained that when the scene is scratched onto the casement of the pocketknife, it is rubbed with India ink and then wiped off again revealing the etching. Klem knew how the process worked but allowed him the dignity to explain it.

"All items come with a leather case to protect it. If it ever is fading and has to be reinked, you can either send it to here or come back, and I will do it for you for no charge."

Klem took the pocketknife in his hands, turning it over and over to look at the details. It was true perfection and felt so good in his hand. Jane looked not at the item, but in Klem's steel blue eyes, which were absorbing every detail of the object in his rough hands. Jane glanced at the store keeper, and when he caught her eye, she said, "*Sold!*"

"Jane," Klem said quietly to only her, "You don't even know the cost."

With a simple loving hand on top of his, she said, "I don't care. You are my soul mate."

Klem knew from that point on, he would always keep it in his pocket to remember this awesome visit with Jane.

The rest of the evening included more strolling along the sidewalks. Toward dusk, the gas streetlights became illuminated giving off their warm yellow glow.

Klem and Jane decided to freshen up a little back at the bed and breakfast. As they walked down the hallway, they paused at each guestroom door to read the names of each room. They remembered theirs was called the "Puffin Room." Other rooms were "The Captain's Room," "Whale Watch," and "The Sand Piper."

In their bathroom, Klem splashed some cool water on his face, while Jane refreshed her pink lipstick and fussed a little with her hair in front of the dressing room mirror. Still seated, she turned to Klem and said, "Hey, hunk! How about you take your woman out for a drink? And I'll let you tell me how pretty I look."

With an invitation like that from Jane, Klem couldn't refuse. They decided to have a drink at Dan's. Dan's had seating on the front porch, and it had a view of their bed and breakfast from across the street. Jane had some sweet, white sparkling wine and Klem had a mix drink called a "rusty nail." Eventually, the cool night was setting in, and Jane had a few goose bumps starting to appear on her bare shoulders. She quietly pulled her wrap over them hoping this would not mean an end to their evening.

Klem noticed her movement and even though he would have wanted to linger on that porch with Jane, his body was getting tired.

"Well, darling, this surely was pleasant, but I guess you might be getting cold and that guestroom might be calling me right about now."

And with that, they pulled their chairs from the little round table and went back to their home away from home.

Just as they re-entered the living room, they heard a stately musical sound flowing from the far corner of the room. The welcoming came from a seven-foot-tall bright brass pendulum grandfather's clock. For over one hundred years, this lovely clock kept pace with the changing times. Every room on the first floor was bathed by its grand, dignified sound. With all the uncertainty of this world, the predictable count of time from this masterpiece was strong and reassuring, like a child finding a loving, guiding hand from a parent when crossing a street. All is well with the world again.

Chapter 21

After All These Years

BREAKFAST THE NEXT DAY CONSISTED of popovers, a delightful combination taste of sweet rolls and dinner rolls. Lynn and Norris put out a selection of homemade jams and light frostings. Jane and Klem both took some sausages and Canadian bacon to put next to their popovers, making their first meal a hearty one of the day. Klem took a portion of rose hip jam and Jane decided on blueberry.

Everything appeared so easy for them to enjoy. It seemed that the breakfast food was displayed so artistically that it was just meant to be totally enjoyed. The plates were oversized so none of the tasty food would spill over the plate's edge. The popovers were on a cascading food terrace on the center of the buffet table, so that each delicate shape would not be compromised. The breakfast meats were the next in order.

Each table had its own silver pots of flavored coffee and hot water for herbal teas. A small selection of teas was found in a wooden box. Its lid had a simple carving—an ocean wave similar to the carving on the mantle of the fireplace. Some of the guests took their plates outside unto the porch where they could also enjoy the early morning activity of tourists strolling past. The oval tables inside had freshly pressed light blue linen table clothes with matching napkins of the same order. The porch tables were round and a little smaller than the ones in the dining room. They were white wicker, having glass tops, and the accompanying chairs had comfortable bold white and green striped cushions.

At the table next to Klem and Jane was a couple at least fifteen years older than them. They were truly enjoying the morning and their first meal of their day. Upon glancing their way, Jane could see that they were not engaged in any conversations. Both husband and wife helped the other with a napkin or pouring their coffee. It seemed so natural for them and not embarrassed by the help from the other. The fact was that helping each other was an expression of their unspoken and mutual love. Maybe the sensual thrills of their early years have been enjoyed and are now just memories, but the mature sharing of a simple breakfast was their lovemaking.

"Klem, without turning around, can you casually look to your left? There is the cutest older couple having breakfast. Do you think we will be like them someday?"

Klem turned to view the older couple enjoying the sweet rolls and ham. "You mean, will I have to help you open up the little non-dairy cream cup?"

Not too amused, Jane replied, "Klem, you do that already! No, I mean, will we still be in love and want to have each other's company?"

Klem noted a little seriousness in Jane's beautiful hazel eyes. "Of course, dearest. This is our perfect moment right now, and I am planning on having many more of these."

To lighten Jane's concern, Klem went on to say, "I have some good news for you, Jane. This very morning, and after careful consideration, I have decided to renew your contract!"

"Mr. Watercrest, not that I am opposed to my contract renewal with you, but why do you think that I have no say in this matter?"

After this reply, Jane reassured Klem in the most feminine way she could, considering where they were that is, in such a respectable and public place. Looking into Klem's eyes, Jane quietly slipped off her right shoe using her left foot. Keeping Klem's gaze fixed with hers, she reached across the breakfast table and took both of Klem's outstretched hands into hers. Without the slightest change in her expression, Jane found Klem's leg under the table with her bare toe. She followed it up under his pant leg. Inch by inch, with a little toe wiggles, she reached up excitingly far and into his lap.

Klem was most proud of his little lady and did not want her to stop, but had no idea what in the world to say about her playful maneuver. So, in doubt of what to do, Klem borrowed some time and went for a drink of his ice water. With what was happening under the table, Klem took a much larger swig of the water than he planned, catching an ice cube in his throat. Instead of cold, the ice cube felt hot as it slowly went down, but not as hot as his heart was for her love at this moment.

"Why Klem, dear, what could possibly be the matter? You appear quite flushed. Should I do something for you?"

After another encore, Jane tapped her naked foot around to find her shoe tipped on its side under the table. She silently reshoed her foot feeling very pleased with herself.

"Darling, maybe you need to take your little lady for a nice walk to see the fishing boats leave the harbor for the day. How about it?"

By this time, he was putty in her hands so to speak. Klem pushed his chair from their table and got up feeling like a real man, but having a little weakness in the knees. He took Jane's arm as a manly gesture and quite frankly to get some stability for himself. The sidewalks were lined with red, pink, and white rose hips. Jane bent down a little to take in some of their sweet perfume. Then, a little less graceful, Klem did likewise.

"Someday, my dear wife, we have to make some more jam from these little beauties."

Jane replied, "You use the word *us*. Maybe you really mean *me*, you have gotten a dreadful amount of thorns in your fingers, which then I need to pull out for hours. Speaking of thorns, how are the Cooper boys doing at the lighthouse? Still working hard or hardly working?"

"Funny that you bring their names up. I was just thinking of those two just now when that family crossed the street in front of us. Those boys were running way ahead of their parents without any care. They couldn't wait to get to the waterfront where that beautiful schooner is docked. They reminded me of Link and Jake. Yes, for the last few weeks, they have forgotten about any work. They come almost every day, but soon, they will be getting their bikes back, so who knows? To tell you the truth, whenever they are not around, I miss them a lot. They remind me of myself when I was their age."

Jane was thinking about the Cooper boys's work ethic, "Klem, just how much did you pay them an hour to do all that weeding on the lighthouse property?"

"Oh, we negotiated the dollar amount to where everyone felt it was fine."

"Now, Klem, you have a way of answering without answering. Just how much did you pay those poor boys?"

"Jane, in many ways, it was free child watch that Caroline and I were giving the Cooper parents."

"Klem, how much!"

"It was a little less than three dollars an hour."

"Oh, I see. And how much less?"

Klem knew that she wouldn't let this go unless he spit out the truth. "Well, we settled for fifty cents."

Jane uncoupled her hand from Klem's, stopped quickly, and turned around to face Klem right there on the waterfront sidewalk.

"Klem, they are just children, and you are sixty-five years old for heaven's sake."

"But... but... they agreed."

Jane retorted, "Well, Mr. Generous, *that* is going to change!"

"Goodness gracious, great balls of tar! The boys are more interested in playing on the old rowboat than anything else. You should see them. They're having a ball every day!"

Jane was still thinking. "Well, Klem, I'll let this go because I know you will fix it, and I'll let it go if you take me on that beautiful white schooner. I read about a two-hour tour out to sea and back to do some whale watching. Is it a deal?"

"Yes, my little lady. It's a deal. In fact, I can't wait to smell some fresh salt air and feel the ocean spray on my face."

The schooner ride was just superb. Jane and Klem found outside seating along the aft side. The bench seating was gently curved to match the curve of the ship's gunnel. All the benches were dark-stained teakwood. Klem lightly rubbed his hand along the top of the bench. It felt as smooth as driftwood. After a nautical mile out from the harbor, the engines were cut off, and the four huge white sails were raised to full mast. The only sounds were the sails catching the wind with a light flutter. At that point, Jane and Klem were given the opportunity to enjoy this beautiful solitude over a glass of white semisweet Chardonnay served in tall plastic stemware. Again, God made a perfect moment.

Chapter 22

The Repairs

THE DAYS WERE FEELING A little cooler now that they were approaching the beginning of September. Summer solstice on June 21, the longest day of the year, was now a memory. The fall equinox, September 21, equal hours of day and night, was coming around soon.

Joyce from Youngstown's Marine College had her plan to repair the lighthouse all arranged. As soon as the end of this week, college juniors would be arriving to start various renovation tasks. They were an eager group of four lads and four women. Besides the eight students, the college paid for a professional foreman to oversee the scaffold building and stucco repair. The entire lighthouse would be surrounded by the scaffolding framework, right up to the lamphouse at the top.

Joyce met Klem once again, this time at Gray Cliff Light, two days before the group arrived at the repair site. She wanted to make Klem feel somewhat involved in the process.

"Klem, how's it going? Can you believe that were here already? It seemed like only yesterday that we met at your home earlier this summer. Can I use this picnic bench to lay out the plans for the renovation? See here, we will need to use scaffolding on the outside, but inside, the winding staircase is in fine shape except for painting. I plan to have one of the students paint the steps, while the others do the scraping just before the painter starts coming down from the top. Also, I would like to restore the iron plaque and cornerstone. We have a glass guy who is volunteering his time and money to replace the one cracked window panel at the top. That would be the southeast side. How does it sound so far, Klem?"

Klem felt his age creeping up on him. Here the younger generations were going to restore his light—younger generations with smooth skin over youthful muscles and all so full of energy. All Klem could do was to stand and look in silence as Joyce went on through the details. Just then, he felt a warm touch on his back.

"Klem, darling," it was Jane, "I brought your fleece-lined windbreaker. It's getting a little nippy up here on the hill."

"Thanks, Hun. I guess I might just be getting in the way here. Maybe I'll go home for a second cup of coffee."

"Sounds good, Klem. Let's let the pros do their thing. Of course, knowing you, you will be visiting several times a day to check on the progress and offer any suggestions you may have."

Klem answered a simple "yes" as they turned toward the village, this time, not only holding hands but also with their slightly wrinkled arms around each other's waist.

Chapter 23

A Bump in the Road

WITHIN A WEEK, THE SCAFFOLDING was in place surrounding the entire light, and scraping had progressed efficiently both inside and outside. Painting would soon commence. As Jane had correctly predicted, Klem stood by every day, sometimes the entire day.

Many of the villagers joined Klem, bringing their lawn chairs to sit nearby each other. From any angle, one could see spectators's fingers pointing upward in one direction or another as they talked. When the sun moved around the lighthouse, so likewise moved the group. Lifting their chairs off the ground keeping their derrieres still half in the chairs, they all looked like a mass of hermit crabs crawling along the grass.

Starting into the second week, Joyce felt she needed to pay Klem a visit at his house. She stayed at the sight each day fielding questions from the workers and making sure there was enough bottled water and packaged food; but this morning was different.

"Hi, Klem. I hope you are pleased with the reconstruction so far. We have stayed on schedule up to this point."

Joyce stopped there to wait for Klem's response. Klem nodded his head in agreement but said nothing quite yet. He was trying to measure the reason for her unexpected early morning visit to his home.

"Klem, late last night, I got a telephone call from a man named Thomas, a building inspector for the state. He informed me that the original kerosene lamp could not be used anymore. We will have to

117

remove the lamp and the Fresnel lens and install an electric beacon lamp. He said that it would be even more powerful and will still rotate like the old kerosene wick lamp. It is an OSHA regulation. Kerosene is a fire hazard and gives off dangerous fumes."

After a few moments to compose himself, Klem managed to reply, "A fire hazard? What is there to catch on fire? Gives off dangerous fumes? If that is the case, I should be dead years ago!"

Joyce knew this was not going to sit well with poor old Klem who was pretty set in his ways.

"Klem, we have the money to disassemble the Fresnel lens and reassemble it in the gift shop. It will have a prominent place where visitors can see it up close. It truly is a thing of beauty, and I will not allow it to be stored away somewhere. In fact, being in the gift shop, more people will have access to it. You know, those visitors who would not be able to climb the lighthouse to the top, will even be able to touch it."

Klem may have been stubborn, but was a reasonable man as well. He knew this was a futile battle to even start. Joyce felt this was one hurdle currently out of the way, but now, she had to lay another one on Klem. Joyce continued, "During the time that the Fresnel lens is taken down and the new electric lamp is put into place, of course, there will not be any light coming from the Gray Cliff Light. This part of the project will take about three to four weeks. I know this is most unfortunate, but it cannot be avoided. Klem, are you okay with this?"

"Well, Joyce, I certainly was hoping for an uninterrupted working light, but it is what it is. Thank you, Joyce, for telling me face to face. You and I both know that this would not have to be approved by me but you certainly extended a nice courtesy to me... much appreciated."

Joyce stood up from the table and shaking his hand to say good-bye she said, "Klem, you are a good man. If it wasn't for you, this lighthouse may have been in such disrepair that it may have been torn down years ago. See you at the site a little later?"

Chapter 24

Our Own Problems

IT WASN'T UNTIL LATE MORNING that Klem walked up to the recon-struction site, and as he came across a cluster of wild blueberry bushes, he decided to sample a few nicely ripe ones.

Klem said to himself and to God, "Gosh, there is certainly nothing like wild Maine blueberries!"

After a few samplings, Klem went further into the thicket tasting as he went along. "Goodness gracious, they get sweeter the further I go into these beauties. Why haven't I tried these before?"

Klem was probably there for a half an hour getting his tongue a little purple along the way. Little did he know, however, he picked up a little pesky visitor. It wasn't until Klem found his lawn chair seat at the base of the lighthouse that he noticed a deer tick on his right leg. The parasite was busy burrowing most of the way into his flesh.

"Darn thing anyway," Klem said to himself, "Why did our good Lord make ticks?"

Against his better judgment, Klem pulled out his old, rather dirty, pocketknife and started to dig it out from his leg. It was deeper than Klem first thought, and it was already gorged and large as it was having its meal on his blood.

While digging out the darn pest, Klem said under his breath, "I probably should have used my new pocket knife Jane bought me from Big Harbor, but I left it on top of my bedroom dresser."

119

Klem tried to make some small talk with Joyce who stopped for a few minutes to down some bottled water. But his leg was getting swollen, red, and hot, a sure sign that infection was setting in. After exchanging a few niceties with her, Klem excused himself and started home.

Chapter 25

A Disaster Waiting to Happen

THAT EVENING, THE TEMPERATURE STAYED warmer than usual. Sometimes, that brings children outside to play, knowing that school is soon to begin again, and it's not good to waste time indoors. There will be enough of that while sitting in the classrooms. The Cooper boys were no exception. After supper, the boys, Link and Jake, planned a wonderful way to end their summer vacation.

Picking up the boys's dinner plates but pausing for a moment before going into the kitchen, Mrs. Cooper said, "Boys, how come you two are racing through your dinner so fast? Is it because you can't wait to see Pastor Dell and start your confirmation classes?"

"What? What? What?" The boys responded in chorus with shock and helplessness in their voices.

"Now, your Dad and I have talked about this to you many times. Don't tell us you forgot because neither one of us will believe it. Now, go upstairs, wash your faces, and get your Bibles. We will be leaving in a few minutes."

Mr. Cooper was just settling down in front of the television and said, "Honey, do you want me to go with you and the boys?"

"No, of course not! You just sit there and enjoy *The Price Is Right*. I just have enough time to clean up the kitchen before I leave!"

For a fleeting second, Mr. Cooper felt relieved, but the reality of marriage responsibilities kicked in.

"I think you are being sarcastic, Honey?"

Mr. Cooper threw in the "Honey" part whenever he thought it would help.

"Put on a clean shirt dear, after all we are going to church. Pastor wants us there at 7:00 p.m. for an informational meeting before his class starts. After the meeting, we can leave the kids and then pick them up later. Pastor Dell said that the class would be over at 8:30 p.m."

Jake and Link's minds were racing at top speed, that is, "top speed" for two twelve year olds whose evening just got changed for the very worst. While sharing the bathroom pedestal sink together, with both faces partway in the sink bowl, a plan was emerging to save their evening. Link gave birth to the plan, and as usual, his brother bought into it.

With faces washed and dried, both jumped down the stairs, two at a time.

Link decided that he could pull this off much better than Jake, so in a most nonchalant voice and manner, Link said casually to their parents, "Say, Mom and Dad, being the fact that you have to take us to church, how about we save you the time and after class we will walk home?"

"That sounds good to me," Mr. Cooper replied.

Of course, he was thinking of salvaging some of his evening television viewing. So in the family sedan, they went with Jake and Link winking at each other in the backseat. Driving the one-mile distance to Our Lord's Lutheran Church only took a short time, but Mrs. Cooper pondered their willingness to walk home, just to save some time for her and hubby.

"You know, Honey," Mrs. Cooper said, as she pulled down the car visor to shield her eyes from the setting sun. "I think our little boys there in the backseat are finally growing up. They are thinking about someone else instead of always themselves."

Mr. Cooper nodded in agreement. He was thinking more about his programs that he will miss on TV.

The Cooper family arrived at the church parking lot on time. They saw the pastor's car and about six others, as they left theirs, and entered from the side entrance.

Pastor Dell welcomed everyone by name as each one found a seat in the classroom.

Looking at his notes, Pastor Dell made a mental roll call and decided that everyone had arrived. He smiled and started, "Our lessons will follow Luther's Small Catechism. It will include the Ten Commandments, the Apostles' Creed, the Lord's Prayer, Baptism, Confession, and Holy Communion. Next year, besides a review of the first year, we will conduct studies such as how us Christians fit into a secular world and our responsibilities, the way we live our lives, problems with illegal drug use, dating, and many more relevant topics. In addition to these studies, each confirmation student will be presenting their religious project in front of the church congregation. Usually, this is open-ended, but it should be on the topic of what was most important or most interesting to each student.

A couple years ago, one of my students did their project on the Ark of the Covenant. He actually built the box using our Bible for his plan. Now, if someone wanted to build Noah's Ark, that would be fine. But hopefully not full size, please."

The pastor went on to say, "Well, this ends the parent information portion of our evening. You parents can go home now, but please be back by 8:30 p.m. to pick up your young adults. Oh, and thank you for your time commitments and your sincere desire to spiritually educate your children."

After this presentation, all the parents left the classroom, leaving their children with Pastor who was still at the front of the room. Jake and Link listened politely to Pastor Dell while he started their first confirmation class. The boys had a glazed look for most of the hour-long lecture. They did sit up in their chairs, completely appalled when they heard "for the first time," that these classes would be for two whole years not just one.

After saying the Lord's Prayer to close the class, Jake and Link were the first to exit the church doors and out into the village street. Their destination was not to go home but to go to the lighthouse. Their plan was unfolding perfectly. Their parents would not be worried about them for another good hour or so.

It was a short run, even with short legs taking them flying over the pavement and then up the dirt path the boys knew so well.

"But what about oars, Link? What are we going to do without oars?"

"Your sea captain has got you covered my first mate. I brought a screwdriver to jimmy open the lighthouse storeroom under the gift shop. I saw some oars there that will work just fine."

Jake thought that if he could be as smart at his brother, Link, especially when both grow up, then he would be truly successful.

The streetlights ended just before the dirt road to the lighthouse, making the path almost hard to even see. Both boys didn't notice how inky black the night was. There was no moon out and no stars to be seen anywhere. As the boys slowed down their running, the lighthouse was just ever so slightly visible in the blackness. Its light totally extinguished for the first time in over one hundred years.

"Link, do you think this is really a good idea? I mean, I am okay, but I don't want you to be scared or anything."

Link reached for his father's screwdriver that he had in his pocket.

"Jake, here goes nothing, with just the right twist of this screw driver, when I say push, you push the door. Okay?"

The storeroom was equally dark, but Link knew where the oars were. So without much time wasted, the boys were running toward the rowboat.

"Good thing Mom didn't have enough time to make this fine seaworthy vessel a meager plant flower box. In with the oars and in goes the crew to places unknown all the way to uncharted waters and luscious wind-swept islands to explore... all for us brave men!"

With that fine speech of encouragement, Jake joined his captain brother, one boy on each side of the boat, lifting it from its summer resting place.

"On my orders men, push this craft down that slope and onto our destiny. The mighty waters await our arrival!"

Actually, Link was very impressed with himself. The way he governed his crew who had complete obedience to him, their fearless captain.

The slope of the hill made the launch easy, and before they knew it, the boys were shoving offshore. Link and Jake, using their oars to dig into the sand, entered into the ever-deepening cold black waters. Link of course was in front with Jake in the back, both facing the same way.

Even in a small village as Port James, sometimes more than one event occurs at the same time, which can change several lives. Earlier this same evening, Klem was sitting in his recliner chair reading but concentrating more to keep his throbbing leg up without raising suspicion. He knew Jane would overreact if she noticed the pain he was trying to hide. Jane decided to go to the upstairs bathroom to check on her makeup. Looking away from her image in the mirror, she saw a small tube sitting on the sink.

"Klem, why is the antibiotic cream out on the bathroom sink? Did you need it for something?"

Klem thought his wife could have been an inspector for the federal government or even a highly sought-after, highly paid, private detective. He knew it wasn't worth his meager effort to keep his condition from her any more.

"Well, Hun, this morning, I was picking some delish blueberries just off the dirt road from the hill. Wouldn't you know it, I picked up a darn deer tick in my leg. But I got most of it out with my pocketknife. End of story."

"Klem, if it is the end of the story, then why are you keeping your leg up? Let me take a look at your surgery job. Come on big guy. Let me pull up your pant leg so I can see."

Jane worked up his pant leg past the problem area.

"Klem, it's all infected! Look at the redness, and your leg is all swollen! Goodness gracious, great balls of mud! Did you clean your pocketknife first? Just look at that wound, it's all full of pus! And it's all hot to the touch! Mr. Watercrest, we are going to the hospital right now!"

By this time, Klem was feeling somewhat dizzy, and as he tried to get up from his chair, the room started to swirl around him, and then everything went white just before he fell to the floor.

Chapter 26

Unsettling Times

Klem arrived at the hospital by ambulance. His first sense of place and time was when the nurses were taking him off the gurney and onto a hospital bed.

A few minutes later, the attending nurse saw Klem's eyes open a little when she adjusted his pillow. She called to the other nurse just outside his hospital room door.

"Help, Barb, I think I finally see life in here!"

Head Nurse Barb came in to start some saline solution intravenously into his arm. Barb checked Klem's pupils and then asked, "Mr. Watercrest, can you hear me? Do you know what happened to you? Do you know where you are? Do you know what date it is?"

Klem answered, "Where is Jane? Can you please tell me where is Jane, my wife?"

Barb continued, "Of course, Mr. Watercrest. Just let me assess your condition first. Do you know what today's date is?"

Klem answered truthfully although rather gruffly for him. "If you don't know what date it is today, then you and I ought to change places. Where is my wife?"

With that, Barb left the room and saw that Jane was just outside the door to the room, waiting in the hall to see Klem. She thought Klem was beyond earshot and said to Jane, "Is that the way your husband usually is? I mean, I just wanted to know if he is in pain or what. He was pretty gruff with me."

Jane ignored her comment and went into Klem's room.

"How are you feeling darling? I was talking with the emergency room doctor in charge. His name is Dr. Moore. He said that they have started antibiotics in your intravenous. Good Lord, Klem. You scared me. From now on, if you are feeling bad or sick, just let me know. Okay?"

Klem answered weakly, "I don't like that nurse."

A few hours later, around 4:00 p.m., the Emergency Room doctor came into Klem's room.

"Hello, Mr. Watercrest. I am Dr. Moore. How are you feeling this evening?"

Klem felt like "death warmed over," but wanted out of that place as soon as possible.

"Hello, Dr. Moore. I feel just peachy. Can you release me?"

The good doctor thought for a few minutes while reading Klem's medical reports at the foot of the bed.

"Well, sir, we can't do anything more for you than if you were home. As soon as the intravenous is done, we can send you home with oral penicillin. Take three each day for fourteen days and monitor that leg. Try to keep it up as much as possible, and as soon as you get home, I want you to stay in bed for three days. Drink plenty of liquids and rest, rest, rest. If you promise you will do this, I'll sign your release papers right now. Oh of course, if the leg doesn't improve, I want you to see your general practitioner. It's Dr. Bentley, right? I will send your medical reports to him so he has a record."

Klem said, "I will do what you say doctor, and God bless. I like you."

By the time Jane got Klem back home and in bed, word got around that the Cooper boys were missing. Mr. Cooper contacted the police and started a walking search in the village.

Mrs. Cooper knew she needed to get to the lighthouse. Once on the dirt path, she was practically feeling her way through the stark darkness by shuffling her feet step by step. Her entire world then fell apart when she got to where the rowboat should have been. Falling to her knees in the cold mud, she knew that Link and Jake had taken the boat out instead of coming straight home.

"Why, oh, why didn't I make a flower planter out of... Oh God, please bring my boys back to me... Please God!"

By this time, clouds were swirling viciously in circles, and the cold wind was picking up, blowing from the sea. Still, there were no stars or moon, just a thick black, cold nightmare that engulfed her surroundings and her soul.

House to house, family to family, word continued to travel, carrying its terrible message of two missing boys. Trish hung up her phone after getting the horrible message from Hank. She tried desperately to make her mind think clearly. Not feeling very well over the past few days, she knew that she would not be of much help to join an outside search. Sarah thought that she should at least call Pastor Dell and inform him. With shaking fingers, she dialed the church office, believing he would still be there.

"Pastor, I need to tell you that the Cooper boys are missing. They must have gone somewhere after your class was over. I have this awful feeling that they are in some terrible trouble."

Pastor thanked her for letting him know, hung up the phone and, since he was still in his church office, went into the sanctuary to pray.

"Dear God, Father Almighty and all-knowing God, please be with Link and Jake. Please guide them home safely no matter where they are now..."

The good Pastor continued his pleads with God, kneeling at the communion railing. He didn't take the time to turn on any lights. With the glow of the eternal candle, he could see the stained-glass window. This same window that depicted a sailboat almost lost at sea and the lighthouse far away on a rock cliff searching for life.

When 10:30 p.m. came, Jane learned about the boys when she saw the search party going down the street. Tom left the search group just a few moments to walk up to Jane's house and tell her of the news. Knowing that Klem would want to know too, she left the porch and went back inside. She went upstairs to their bedroom wondering if Klem was asleep. Knocking lightly on the door, she entered.

"Klem, are you awake? I need to tell you that Jake and Link are missing now for a few hours, maybe more. People are looking, but there is no sign of them so far."

"Oh, God," Klem answered. "Those boys have stolen my heart... Oh, God."

"Now, Klem, you need to get some rest. You promised Dr. Moore that you will follow his direction for your recuperation. Now, lie back down, dear. So as not to disturb you, I am going to sleep in the recliner downstairs. I'm also going to take our windup alarm clock with me and set it for when you need to take your next antibiotic pill."

Reclining his head on the pillow, Klem said, "Thanks, Jane. You take good care of me."

Jane thought for a moment, looking at her sick husband. She remembered something that could be helpful and went to the bedroom closet and picked up a small silver bell the grandchildren like to play with.

"Now, Klem," she said as she whispered into his ear, "Don't get used to this, but if you need me for anything, ring the bell and I will come up."

Chapter 27

Faith amidst the Perils, Part 1

By this time, the storm at sea was pushing the little rowboat back and forth like a toy. Link and Jake were both terrified and freely admitted this to each other. The boys had been out among the cold dark waves for three hours, just barely keeping afloat. Their striped short sleeve shirts and blue jeans were soaked with unending sprays of angry seawater. Their clothes clung to their little bodies giving them no warmth. Several times, the tiny vessel with its precious cargo nearly capsized into the depths. The little boys were crying but kept on paddling toward what they thought to be the shore. They truly couldn't tell between the waves and the sky, both were black and cold. Their world was mean and vicious. Its power against them was no match for the failing boys.

Behind him, Link heard Jake calling out among his tears for their mommy. Above the crashing sound of the waves, he yelled out to his brother in total desperation, "Jake, can you say a prayer for us, please… please… please? Jake, say a prayer, please!"

Above the crashing sounds, Link heard his brother's prayer, a prayer from a little child's voice, a prayer for both of them, "Now, I lay me down to sleep…"

At that point, a huge rogue wave spilled into the boat.

Chapter 28

Faith amidst the Perils, Part 2

KLEM LAID IN HIS BED sweating but shaking at the same time. His sheets were soaking wet from his uncontrollable perspiration. He had prayed for the boys for over an hour but felt God was calling him to do what He needed Klem to do. Klem carefully rolled from his back to his side, and as silently as possible, he moved his feet to the floor and stood upright. Half walking, half crawling, Klem maneuvered to the closet and found a dry set of clothes to put on. Step by painful step, he got down the stairs hanging on the banister handrail. Going past Jane who was now asleep on the living room recliner chair, he knew he had to exit his house from the back door. As Klem placed his hands on the door, he said a simple payer.

"Please God, give me the strength."

Klem knew with absolute certainty that Jake and Link went out on the water with the boat by the lighthouse. He also knew that without the guiding light from the top of his lighthouse, they would never find their way back. The sea was like that. It could turn violent within minutes and countless times had swallowed up seaworthy vessels, cargo, and lives, sending it all to the depths. But now, his lighthouse was dark, and its guiding beam was nonexistent. All the parts of the lighthouse were still at the top, the Fresnel lens, the kerosene well, and its wick, all there but shut off, waiting for its replacement.

Klem felt for his long wooden stick matches that were in his breast pocket and went out into the rain, letting the door close silently behind him. The wind immediately pushed him off balance, as he headed up to find the dirt path. The rain soaked his hair within seconds; his hands were already cold. He knew he had to keep the wooden matches dry in his pocket. Klem needed to make his lighthouse illuminate just once more, even if there was just enough kerosene left on the wick for a few seconds of light.

The village street ended, and Klem continued on the dirt path, only a few tenths of a mile to his lighthouse. His feet stumbled; mud covered his pants. What seemed to be hours later, he finally touched the door to the lighthouse. It was unlocked. Before opening it, he saw the empty spot now full of mud, where the rowboat had been. Just beyond, he could vaguely make out the form of the boys's mother. She was kneeling, shaking, and mouthing pleading words to God, words he could not make out. Her hair was mixed with sand and rain, stuck to her head, covering most of her face.

He desperately wanted to go to her and comfort her the best he could, but he couldn't afford any precious time; instead, he opened the lighthouse door. Hopelessly, Klem looked up at the dark winding staircase above his head. He had to reach the top.

Chapter 29

Faith amidst the Perils, Part 3

LINK AND JAKE WERE HELPLESSLY lost, and their boat had a foot of water in the bottom. Both the boys's little frame and muscles were aching to stop paddling, but they struggled on, trying to find shore. Link weakly called to Jake, hoping he could hear him above the crashing waves and wind.

"Jake, can you think of a church song? One that would help us... anyone? If you sing, I might be able to hear you and join you. Jake, we really need a church song, a hymn... anything... Jake... anything... Jake? Please? Jake?"

The wooden paddles although smooth were rubbing the top layers of their little hands so much that the handles were red with their pulsating blood. The saltwater made piercing stings like knives aggravating the pain. Jake summoned the best of his short memory from church and faintly started his prayer hymn,

> Eternal Father, Strong to save
> Whose arm has bound the restless waves
> Who bidd'st the mighty ocean deep
> Its own appointed limits keep,
> O hear us when we cry to thee,
> For those in peril on the sea.[1]

---

[1] William Whiting, *Eternal Father, Strong to Save*(1860), Public Domain

Chapter 30

I am the Light and the Way

KLEM COULD FEEL THE THROBBING all through his body, not just his leg. One by one, each step up, more painful than the one before, he continued the ascent. The winding staircase seemed to multiply endlessly. Not that he could see in the darkness, but he knew in his weakness, the steps would look like they were swirling around his head. He held onto the iron railing, praying that he wouldn't fall. One slip would certainly send him cascading down to the first step.

His head was pounding in tempo with his pulsating heart. His mouth was dry, as both legs started to cramp like a rope wound tightly around his muscles.

"It has to be only a few more steps. Lord, please continue to be with me, only a few more steps for the boys."

Unknown to Klem's fading mind, the infection now was starting to cloud his brain. Klem had thirty more steps to go.

"God, please give me the strength," Klem pleaded.

He fought the powerful temptation to sit on the step he was on just to rest a short time, but he knew that he would pass out into a deep sleep.

"Our Father who art in heaven..." Klem prayed as he pushed his muscles beyond their limits.

After twenty excruciating minutes, Klem felt a thin flow of air against his face. He knew it was coming from the cracked glass window at the lamphouse. He had finally made it to the top. Now with one strike of his match against the lighthouse wall, the match lit up, just a few inches from the lighthouse wick and then faded away, uselessly without completing its task. In the cold darkness, Klem yielded to his failing strength and slumped to the floor.

In that instant of time, just before Klem succumbed to the floor, Jake and Link saw the bright guiding beacon of the lighthouse, piercing through the waves and rain. If they had continued in the direction they were paddling, they would have gone deeper into the sea. With all their might, they paddled the boat around in the direction of the light. A real message of salvation came to Link and Jake. They could, they would, with the last of their meager strength make it back to shore.

Pastor Dell, at this same wonderful moment, looked up from his prayers and saw the message of God right in front of him. There in the solitude of the church's darkness, the guiding light from the stained-glass lighthouse radiated for a few quick seconds. It focused its guiding beam on the boat among the waves and rain depicted in the scene. Shivering from this heavenly message, Pastor Dell ran outside into the rain. There were no stars, no moon, and no other light to explain what he experienced inside his church.

Klem awoke a few minutes later; his wooden matches lying on the lamphouse floor in a puddle of water, totally useless. With bitter tears streaming down his face, in the darkness, he slowly made the descent down the winding stairs.

"How could God fail me?" Klem asked out loud. He tried so hard to light the way for the boys. No, God did not fail him. He himself failed Link and Jake. He should have known better than to infect himself with his old pocket knife. He could have made it to the top with ease like he did countless times before. He would not have fainted just before lighting the wick.

Klem finally made it down to the last step. He felt the weight of his whole community on his shoulders. There at the landing was Jane to catch him as he fell into her arms.

Epilogue

In God We Trust

"This is the day that the Lord has made. Let us rejoice and be glad in it!"

There was absolutely no earthly or scientific explanation for the lighthouse to broadcast its bright and powerful beacon the way it did that one night. Some said that the beam lasted for almost three whole minutes, cascading two whole miles to sea.

The same was true for the stained-glass window at the church. Miracles happen, and that is what Pastor Dell prayed for. Sometimes, God uses us mortals on Earth to carry out miracles through our prayers. We may not know that we will be God's hand to deliver a miracle, but we should ask God that we are both worthy and diligent to do so.

So once again, town life goes on. Seasons change, and summer plants are put safely inside for the winter. Storm doors and shutters are used again to keep out the chilly weather. There are wonderful villages and towns scattered all over our country and beyond, places of living, a place to work, and a place to call home.

But the places in which we live do not make entirely the joy in one's life. The true joy comes from helping others and appreciating every gift from God, large and small. Jane and Klem have a framed print in their living room that reads, "Enjoy the little things in life for someday you will realize they were the big things."

Klem adds to that "enjoy people, help people, and cherish all good relationships. They are also God's blessings for us."

Trish died a year later of cancer, with her husband Hank by her bedside. She left this world a mere ninety-four pounds, but her soul flew into the waiting, loving arms of Jesus himself.

After finishing high school, Jake entered the Lutheran Seminary and became a Pastor of a large congregation in Massachusetts. He and his wife, Joan, have two boys and three girls. His brother, Link pursued his love of the sea and works as an offshore man at a thriving seaport in Rhode Island.

As for Klem, he fully recovered from his infection. He and Jane can be seen sharing both their early and evening walks through town, holding hands, and stopping occasionally to chat with neighbors, enjoying God's creation all around them. They are now totally retired and take little "getaways" whenever they can.

About the Author

JAY GREW UP IN A small upper New York State village of Spencerport. He lives with his wife, Alicia, and a little puppy named Carly. They do volunteer work in their community as well as with their church. They have been blessed with three children and seven grandchildren, who have fun building memories of all kinds when they get together.

CPSIA information can be obtained
at www.ICGtesting.com
Printed in the USA
BVOW09s2002260418

514540BV00001BA/78/P